"Why don't you just lock me in your bedroom so you'll have me right where you want me?"

His gaze snapped to hers and she realized what she'd said. It shouldn't have been a big deal. It should have just been a friendly joke, poking fun at his insistence on keeping such a close eye on her.

But that *thing* between them rose up like a dragon, assaulting them with the burning fire of lust. Victoria knew her cheeks were red with embarrassment.

Brody, on the other hand, was staring at her as if she'd just stripped naked in front of him or something.

She had no idea how long they stood there silently with her words between them.

She watched emotions chase each other across his face—surprise, lust, even curiosity. Was he wondering what it would be like to make love with her?

Because that's exactly what she couldn't get out of her mind.

MALLORY KANE

the HEART *of* BRODY McQUADE

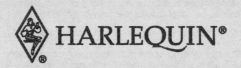

HARLEQUIN®

TORONTO • NEW YORK • LONDON
AMSTERDAM • PARIS • SYDNEY • HAMBURG
STOCKHOLM • ATHENS • TOKYO • MILAN • MADRID
PRAGUE • WARSAW • BUDAPEST • AUCKLAND

To Delores and Rita—here we go again.

ISBN-13: 978-0-373-69336-8
ISBN-10:   0-373-69336-2

THE HEART OF BRODY MCQUADE

Copyright © 2008 by Rickey R. Mallory

ABOUT THE AUTHOR

Mallory Kane credits her love of books to her mother, a librarian, who taught her that books are a precious resource and should be treated with loving respect. Her father and grandfather were steeped in the southern tradition of oral history, and could hold an audience spellbound for hours with their storytelling skills. Mallory aspires to be as good a storyteller as her father.

She loves romantic suspense with dangerous heroes and dauntless heroines, and often uses her medical background to add an extra dose of intrigue to her books. Another fascination that she enjoys exploring in her reading and writing is the infinite capacity of the brain to adapt and develop higher skills.

Mallory lives in Mississippi with her computer-genius husband, their two fascinating cats, and, at current count, seven computers.

She loves to hear from readers. You can write her at rickey_m@bellsouth.net or c/o Harlequin Books, 233 Broadway, Suite 1001, New York, NY 10279.

Books by Mallory Kane

HARLEQUIN INTRIGUE

738—BODYGUARD/HUSBAND*
789—BULLETPROOF BILLIONAIRE
809—A PROTECTED WITNESS*
863—SEEKING ASYLUM*
899—LULLABIES AND LIES*
927—COVERT MAKEOVER
965—SIX-GUN INVESTIGATION
1021—A FATHER'S SACRIFICE*
1037—SILENT GUARDIAN
1069—THE HEART OF BRODY MCQUADE

*Ultimate Agents

CAST OF CHARACTERS

Lt. Brody McQuade—The no-nonsense Head of the Rangers' Unsolved Crimes Unit in San Antonio has been assigned to solve a series of break-ins and killings in wealthy Cantara Hills. But his real agenda is uncovering the truth behind his sister's death.

Victoria Kirkland—The successful attorney was at odds with Brody McQuade after she defended a suspect implicated in his sister's death.

Sgt. Egan Caldwell—This Ranger is married to the badge.

Sgt. Hayes Granger—The third member of the Unsolved Crimes Unit team resents the rich life because of his rough upbringing.

Kimberly McQuade—Was Brody's younger sister murdered because of what she learned as a political intern?

Carlson Woodward—The biological son of Brody's foster parents has always been jealous of Brody's accomplishments. But would he stoop to murder to get back at Brody?

Kenneth Sutton—The powerful and ambitious chairman of the city board, he argued with Kimberly the night she was killed, making him a prime suspect in her death.

Tammy Sutton—The perfect trophy wife for a powerful politician on his way up, Tammy's cool composure and sultry looks hide her manipulative, scheming brain.

Vincent Montoya—Chauffeur to Kenneth Sutton, his sharp eyes miss nothing.

Miles Landis—Young and irresponsible, Miles is half-brother to heiress Taylor Landis and next in line to inherit millions. He's also a compulsive gambler in deep debt.

Prologue

Christmas Eve

Lieutenant Brody McQuade, Texas Ranger, looked at the ornate casket for the first time since he'd walked into the quiet chapel. His heart twisted with pain so severe he couldn't breathe. That was his baby sister beneath that blanket of pink and white poinsettias. *Kimmie.*

Ever since he could remember, his mom had drilled into him that Kimberly was his responsibility.

If anything ever happens to us... Those words weren't just empty motherisms. His parents had been thrill-seekers, and wealthy enough to pursue their dangerous hobbies.

A pipe organ's dulcet tones swelled. Brody's throat closed and his shoulders bowed as if they could shield his heart from deeper pain. Out of habit he straightened them. He was a Texas Ranger and Rangers were always strong and straight— dependable and responsible.

Next to him, Sergeant Hayes Keller turned his head slightly. "You all right?" he whispered.

Brody lifted his chin. No way could he let Hayes or the third Ranger on the pew, Egan Caldwell, know the shape he was in. He was their superior officer. His responsibility to them and to the Rangers went beyond personal feelings.

Ah, dammit, Kimmie. What were you doing in that car without your seat belt on? He stared at his hands and pretended the blurriness in his eyes wasn't tears.

Hayes nudged him.

"The service is over, Brody. Let's go."

He raised his head. The music had stopped. In the silence he heard clothes rustle and a few quiet coughs. Everyone was waiting for him to make the first move.

He stood, bitter nausea clogging his throat. Why the hell hadn't he insisted on a private service? He felt the stares from the people in the chapel—most of whom could have prevented this tragedy if they'd paused in their partying and drinking for one second.

He approached the casket. He reached out a hand, but he couldn't bring himself to actually touch the polished surface.

"Bye, Kimmie," he whispered hoarsely. "I swear I'll put the bastard who did this away for the rest of his worthless life."

He felt a touch on his shoulder.

He looked up. It was Caroline Stallings, the socialite who'd let Kimmie die. What kind of woman drove with the top down three days before Christmas? And let a passenger ride with no seat belt?

"Lieutenant McQuade, please accept my condolences. I feel so bad about what happened."

He took in her pale face and bruised forehead. It was all he could do to rein in the anger that churned in his gut. He met her gaze, gleaning a grim satisfaction when her eyes widened with apprehension. "Thanks," was all he could manage.

With Egan and Hayes behind him, he navigated through the crush of attendees, most of whom he'd only met in the past three days as he'd interrogated them about Kimberly's death.

He'd had no idea that interning on the San Antonio City Board would throw Kimberly into the middle of the city's wealthiest inner circle. Caroline Stallings was on the board, and maybe that explained it. Kimberly had admired Caroline, had in fact raved about her.

But there was something fishy about the hit-and-run crash that had taken his sister's life, and before he got through with them, he planned to unearth all these Cantara Hills trust-fund babies' dirty little secrets.

Just as he reached the rear door he saw a familiar, squir-relly face. Gary Zelke, the SOB who had drunkenly slammed into Caroline Stallings's vintage Corvette.

Frustration, grief and anger roiled inside him like a toxic stew. He eased past a tall blonde who smelled like money and roses, and confronted the little twerp.

"What the hell are you doing here?"

Zelke turned white as a sheet. "Just paying my respects."

"Why aren't you in jail? You've got a lot of gall." Brody clenched his fists. His jaw ached. "I ought to—"

"Pardon me."

It was the blonde. Her tailored suit revealed legs that went all the way to the ground. In heels, she came close to his six foot two.

"I'm Victoria Kirkland. We met briefly at the police station the day after the accident."

He frowned, trying to place her. Suddenly the memory hit him. She was Zelke's ambulance-chasing lawyer and a po-tential witness. She'd driven through the intersection seconds before Caroline and Kimberly had.

"*You.* You bailed him out. After the dirt-wad left my sister lying in the street."

Victoria Kirkland flattened her lips and nodded. "Lieutenant, my deepest sympathy goes out to you and your family—"

Brody leveled his famous quelling gaze on her. "But…?"

Her green eyes sparked without faltering, and a tiny quirk of her lips surprised him. She gave him back look for look and her expression clearly said, *Don't even try.*

"*But* I'm Mr. Zelke's attorney. Anything you have to say, you say to me."

Brody ground his teeth. "He killed my sister."

Now her gaze faltered. "He didn't, but I won't argue the point here while you're in mourning."

Brody clenched his fists and his jaw. "Don't do me any favors, Counselor."

"You have my card. Call me and we can discuss the charges you're bringing against my client."

All of Brody's anger and pain transferred itself to the long, cool blonde. Sharp as a stiletto and twice as dangerous. If she were cut she'd probably bleed ice water. Why was she bothering with a two-bit drunk like Zelke?

She wasn't sleeping with him. Hell, she'd eat him alive.

Brody rubbed his eyes and turned away. One thing he knew for sure. When she tangled with *him,* she'd lose, because he had the advantage. Her heart wasn't in it. His was.

He was fighting for justice for his little sister.

Chapter One

Eight months later

"Hey, Caldwell, get up!" Brody McQuade pushed open the door to the second bedroom of the luxury conference suite at the Cantara Hills Country Club. His fellow Ranger was nothing more than an irregular lump under the fancy bedspread.

"Egan!"

The lump stirred. A rude, muffled comment reached Brody's ears. "Let's go. We've got another break-in."

The lump turned into a head with brown hair sticking out every which way. "Another...at the condos?" Egan cursed and sat up, kicking at the bedclothes. He yawned and rubbed his head.

"Yeah. Come on."

Egan squinted at him. "You're already dressed."

Brody didn't respond.

Egan sighed. "I'll catch up. What room?"

"Didn't get particulars. The police are there. Ask at the door." Brody left Egan sitting on the side of his bed with his head in his hands.

Grabbing his holster and hat, Brody stalked out to his Jeep Compass. The whine of police sirens echoed in his ears. He could see flashing blue lights in the near distance, over the Cantara Gardens Condominiums, south of the country club.

Adrenaline pumped through him and he had trouble reining in his impatience on the four-minute drive around the back nine holes of the golf course to the condos' gates. He'd have preferred to sprint across the manicured greens and straightaways. Probably wouldn't take forty seconds if he ran flat out.

But arriving at a crime scene sweaty and wrinkled wasn't the Ranger way. Nor was it Brody's style.

He'd been expecting this. There had been a break-in every month at the condos since January. Seven so far. Two fatalities. Trent Briggs in February, and Gary Zelke three months later, in May.

Deason hadn't mentioned the name of the latest victim. The San Antonio Police Department Detective Sergeant had sounded frantic.

Did that mean they'd had another fatality?

He pulled up to the gate where an SAPD officer waved him through. Normally the residents used a computerized access card to open the gate. He had a master in his pocket.

Pulling up beside a police car, he headed inside. He didn't recognize the officer at the front door, but the young man's eyes lit on the silver star pinned to his shirt pocket and nodded. "Sergeant Deason is waiting for you, sir. In the penthouse."

He raised his eyebrows. *The penthouse.* Victoria Kirkland's apartment. Naturally it had to be her. Anger bubbled up from his chest, hot and noxious as methane gas.

Suck it up, McQuade. Tonight she wasn't the shyster who'd

gotten Kimmie's killer off with nothing but a DUI. Tonight she was a victim. He didn't ask if she'd survived the break-in. If she hadn't, Deason would have told him.

He stepped into the elevator and eyed the button labeled "P." Beside it was a narrow horizontal slot. He inserted the master access card the condos' manager had given him into the slot and pressed the button.

The elevator car rumbled and started climbing, straight to the top. The doors opened into a foyer that could have been the lobby of a fancy hotel, complete with massive vases of flowers, illuminated artworks, and marble floors and columns.

Damn. Victoria Kirkland didn't make *this* kind of money practicing law. She was a trust-fund baby. He should have known.

He pointedly ignored the voice in his head that reminded him that he was, too. His situation was different. For one thing, he was never going to touch the money his careless, carefree parents had placed in trust for Kimmie and him.

As his boot heels clicked on the marble floor, he heard heavier boots on the dark mahogany staircase to his left. The tall, burly detective sergeant, Cal Deason, came down the stairs.

"McQuade," he said, holding out his hand.

Brody shook it briefly. He and Deason had worked together before. They both knew that the Rangers were in charge of this investigation, but Brody was careful to give Deason his full respect and consideration for his position. "What's going on? Have we got a fatality?"

Deason shook his head. "Nope. She was damn lucky."

Brody's gut clenched. Lucky? Yeah. Some people were born lucky. He concentrated on the slight weight of the unique silver badge pinned to his shirt and reminded himself that this wasn't personal.

Personally, he despised the leggy attorney for making good on her promise to get Gary Zelke acquitted of the charge of vehicular manslaughter. But as a Texas Ranger, he was bound to protect her and stop these break-ins and murders.

"Injuries?"

"Bruises on her neck. But other than that, just scared."

So the perp had gotten in. Tried to kill her. That fit the pattern. If he'd succeeded, this would have been the third killing in eight months—if he counted Kimmie's. One murder every three months.

"The guy got past the condo's security alarm system," Deason went on, "just like every other time. But Ms. Kirkland had her own system installed when she moved in." Deason nodded toward the ceiling.

Brody followed his gaze and spotted the security cameras trained on the doors. "You get the tapes?"

Deason nodded. "That's the only camera, and the guy didn't use the front door, but I'll have my guys go through them."

"No. I'll send them to Austin. Sergeant Caldwell will take them."

"I'll have 'em ready."

Deason's words were affable, but Brody detected a note of resentment in his tone. He couldn't blame the homicide sergeant. But Deason knew Brody had no choice. The request for the Rangers to take charge of the investigation had come from the mayor through the governor.

The residents of Cantara Hills had the clout to cover their butts. Once the Rangers had control of the investigation, there'd be no question of conflict of interest.

"I'd appreciate it. How'd the perp get inside?"

Deason shook his head. "My guys are checking. However he did it, he went out the same way. Ms. Kirkland's extra security may have saved her life, but it allowed the perp to get away clean."

"I assume your guys are going over that area with a fine-toothed comb. Give Sergeant Caldwell anything you find. As long as we've got the Rangers' crime lab, we might as well use it. Where is Ms. Kirkland?"

"In the kitchen. She wanted some hot tea."

His mental picture of her modified slightly to add a fragile expensive teacup to her perfectly manicured hand. He'd figured her as a fancy martini type.

"Sergeant Caldwell will be here in a minute to help you process the scene. I'm going to talk to her."

Deason nodded toward his right. "That-a-way. McQuade…"

He turned back.

"She hasn't been processed yet. I told her we could wait until she'd calmed down."

Wealth hath its privileges.

He knew that, too well. What he'd never been able to figure out was why great wealth didn't come packaged with wisdom and responsibility.

If his parents hadn't missed out on the responsibility gene, his and his sister's lives might have taken another path and Kimberly would be alive.

Quelling the urge to clutch at his chest where grief and loneliness still squeezed the life out of his heart, he stepped around a marble column, through a formal dining room and into the kitchen area.

The kitchen was as outrageously opulent as the foyer and

living room. It was more like a balcony than a kitchen, with paned windows running across one entire wall, Mexican quarry tile on the floors and teak lounging furniture taking the place of a table and chairs.

Victoria was sitting on a love seat holding a mug in both hands while a young police officer stood nearby looking bored and awestruck at the same time.

Brody caught his eye. "Crime-scene kit?"

The officer nodded. "Yes, sir. Right here." He toed a metal case at his feet.

"Help them upstairs." He gestured with his head. "Leave the case here."

Victoria looked up. Her mug jerked slightly, even though her pale face didn't change expression. "Lieutenant McQuade. I didn't expect to see you." Her voice was husky.

He bit back a retort. Did she actually think he'd send someone else just because she was the victim? This was his case, and he didn't let anything interfere with a case. "I was available."

She muttered something. It sounded like *Lucky me.*

"Tell me what happened."

She set the mug of tea down on the teak side table. "Can I make you some tea or coffee?"

"No. Tell me what happened."

Her lips compressed into a thin line and she sat back. For the first time he noticed what she was wearing. It was some kind of shiny satiny nightgown with a robe over it. Except that it wasn't exactly a robe. It was black and red and looked Oriental. A kimono? Whatever it was, it and the gown together hardly qualified as clothes. The material of both was so slinky and clingy that he could see the vague outline of her nipples and the V where her thighs met.

Lust speared through him. *Hell*. He swallowed and concentrated on her words.

"I went to bed fairly early, around eleven. I must have gone right to sleep because the next thing I knew something startled me." She lifted the mug and blew across its surface. The satiny fabric whispered and shimmered.

Brody's mouth went dry. Dragging his gaze away from her slender body, he focused on her feet. They were encased in delicate, ivory, open-toed slippers. Her toenails were unpainted—naked.

He shifted his gaze to the windows. "What startled you? A sound?"

"Maybe. I woke up and I knew someone was in my apartment. Sergeant Deason has already asked me all of this."

"Now I'm asking. And trust me, this won't be the last time."

"I'm aware of how investigations work, Lieutenant. I was merely pointing out that you might save yourself some time if you talked to him."

No. You're merely testing to see if you can intimidate me with your wealth and position. He crossed his arms. She was a victim here. As much as she irritated him, he couldn't forget that.

"I've got plenty of time. What happened next?"

Her fingers tightened on the mug. "I sat up and he— whoever it was—grabbed my throat." She closed her eyes. "He pushed me down and flipped me onto my stomach before I could react. Then the security alarm went off."

"It went off after he attacked you?"

"It's my personal security system, not the building's. It trips when a door or a window is breached. It automatically calls the police, then after fifteen seconds, the siren goes off."

"Fifteen seconds? You could be dead in fifteen seconds."

What little color she had in her face drained away. "Th-the theory is that the police get a head start."

"Brilliant theory," Brody muttered. "The condo's security system never went off, just like the other break-ins."

"What does that mean? Are you saying it's one of us?"

He bristled at her words. One of us. As opposed to whom? "Do you mean the residents of Cantara Hills, rather than the rest of San Antonio?"

She angled her head and assessed him. "I mean one of the residents of Cantara Gardens. Lieutenant, should I be talking to someone else? I'm afraid your personal grudge against me might jeopardize this investigation."

"There is absolutely nothing personal about my feelings for you."

"Are you sure? Because it certainly sounds personal."

Brody reined in his rising irritation. She was right. His question had been out of line. She was the victim of a potentially deadly crime. That was all that mattered. The fact that she was instrumental in freeing the drunken weasel who killed his sister had no bearing on this case. Nor did the unfortunate fact that despite himself, he was attracted to her.

"What about Gary and Trent? Do you think it means anything that they're the only two who've been killed?"

And there it was.

The one thing that kept gnawing at his brain and digging at his insides. He couldn't shake the feeling that their deaths had something to do with his sister's death eight months before. His notebook was filled with notes and charts and analyses of every detail of the break-ins and murders—their similarities and their differences.

Everything about the break-ins led back to one undeniable

fact. If he started with the night Kimberly was killed, the fatalities in Cantara Hills were three months apart. December, February, May and now August. The break-ins had started in January. There had been one a month since then. The theory was that the five people who weren't home when the break-ins occurred had been lucky. But Brody had a different theory.

Trent Briggs and Victoria Kirkland had left socialite Taylor Landis's party together that fateful night, just ahead of Caroline and Kimberly. Zelke had left a few minutes after Kimberly. Victoria had passed the intersection just seconds before Zelke plowed into Caroline's Vette and fled the scene of the crime.

Briggs and Zelke had been killed during *break-ins*. And now the last person who'd been near the scene at the critical time that night had been attacked.

And nearly killed.

But Brody didn't want to get into that with her. She'd denied seeing anything that night, and she'd gotten Zelke off with nothing more than leaving the scene of an accident and driving under the influence.

Brody hated her for that. Even though she'd proved that another vehicle had crashed into Caroline's car first. Even though the final coroner's report concluded that Kimberly had already been thrown from the car before Zelke hit it.

"Lieutenant? None of the other break-in victims were attacked, were they? Their apartments were broken into while they were gone." Her eyes glittered and the mug clattered as she set it down. "So why Gary? Why Trent? Why...me?"

Dammit. She was really spooked. Despite his resentment, the hint of tears in her eyes and the faint trembling of her lower lip tugged at his heart.

"The theory is that the others were lucky they weren't home," he said noncommittally.

"It's too much of a coincidence. Trent and I passed that intersection only seconds before Caroline and Kimberly, and then Gary."

"Let's get back to what happened tonight. Now, did you notice anything about your attacker? Was he big? Small? Fat? Skinny?"

"I don't know. His hands maybe. They were strong—big."

"Any scars? Any identifying marks?"

She shook her head without looking at him.

Dammit, he needed something to go on. She was the first—the only one who'd been attacked and lived to tell it. "What about his clothes? Long sleeves? What about smell? After-shave? Cologne? Bad breath?"

Her head still turned back and forth. "I can't tell you anything. I was asleep and then he was there." Her voice quavered.

Brody's frustration built. He planted his feet hip-width apart and crossed his arms over his chest. "So a man broke into your home, found his way to your bedroom and attacked you, and you can't tell me one thing about him? Are you even sure it was a man?"

Victoria opened her mouth, but the retort he expected didn't surface. Instead, she closed her eyes and the corners of her mouth grew white and pinched. "I'm sure it was a man."

"How?"

She glanced up at him. For an instant her green eyes flashed with fear. Then she dropped her gaze. "His breaths sawing in and out in my ear. He sounded—and felt—like a man." She wrapped her arms tightly around herself.

Then she shuddered, and her terror and revulsion reverberated inside him.

"All right. Good. Now stand up. I need to see your neck."

"It's fine."

"That's not your call to make. As an *attorney,* I'd think you'd know that. I need to examine the bruises and process you."

"Process me?"

He cleared his throat impatiently. "Look, Ms. Kirkland. I know you understand procedure. So it'd be helpful if you'd cooperate."

She stood, her green eyes glittering. "I apologize. I'm not trying to be difficult. I seem to be distracted." She lifted her chin, exposing the bruises on her neck.

Irritated because her distress was getting to him, Brody pulled out his cell phone and hit a prerecorded number. "Egan. You upstairs?"

"Yeah. I was going to let you know I was here, but it looked like you and the victim were butting heads, so I left you alone."

"Is there a female officer up there? I want to process Victoria."

"Yeah," Egan said slowly. "A very nice one."

"Send her down." He hung up and pocketed his phone, then retrieved the small green case labeled CSI. Inside he found a disposable digital camera and a small stack of fingerprint paper.

He stood in front of her. In bare feet she seemed a lot smaller than she had at Kimmie's funeral and Zelke's arraignment. Those high heels she always wore added a lot.

"Sir?"

"Yeah," he answered the female voice without turning around. "You're Officer…"

"Martin. Sheila."

"Good. Thanks for coming down." He got the camera ready, then spoke to Victoria.

"Can you lift your hair out of the way?"

She twisted her hair up, holding it with one hand, exposing her slender neck. Ugly black and purple ovals stood out against her creamy skin.

Rage against the bastard who'd attacked her clenched at Brody's insides. He had to quell the urge to touch her marred skin, to soothe it.

What the hell was going on in his head? He didn't soothe victims. His approach was to treat them with respect and detachment. The last thing they needed was to be treated like victims.

It was Kimmie's death. For the past eight months his emotions had been all upside down and backward. Things were getting to him that never had in the past.

In any case, Victoria Kirkland was the last person on earth he should be tempted to comfort. He ignored the supple curve of her neck and concentrated on the bruises.

Moving quickly and efficiently, he snapped several pictures from various angles, instructing her to turn this way and that.

There were obvious similarities between her injuries and those of Zelke and Briggs. The theory that he'd been forming clicked. Their deaths weren't random and neither were the break-ins of unoccupied apartments.

He needed to bounce this off his team. He'd known them both since childhood, but he'd never figured either one of them would amount to much. Egan had always been too bitter about his unfeeling father, and Hayes's home life had better prepared him to be on the other side of the law.

But they'd both grown up to be fine men and fine

Rangers. Egan's practical if surly outlook on life and Hayes's sense of irony had kept Brody grounded these past months. They'd tell him in a heartbeat if his suspicions were off base.

"Officer Martin, how long have you been on the force?" he asked.

"Seven months, sir."

"Ever seen a strangling victim?"

Victoria Kirkland turned her head at the question. What was Lieutenant McQuade doing? "I'd rather not be made a spectacle," she muttered.

"Just stay still. This won't take long."

Victoria closed her eyes and took a long breath. "I don't see the relevance."

He didn't answer her. "Get three or four small fingerprint sheets from the kit," he said to Officer Martin.

"Yes, sir."

"See these markings? They're the same as on the two previous victims. All three were strangled from behind." Brody's voice was detached, his attitude one hundred percent business. But Victoria could feel his finger hovering a millimeter above her skin as he traced the bruises on her neck.

"Yes, sir."

From her voice, Victoria could tell that the young officer was as awestruck as a teenager meeting her favorite rock star.

Not that Victoria blamed her. Brody McQuade was one big hunk of eye candy. All rugged and brooding and intense. The Texas Ranger badge and the in-charge attitude only upped his sex appeal.

At that very instant, his hand slid to her shoulder. His touch was warm and reassuring, until she realized all he was doing was turning her so that her back was to him.

"Hand me the sheets and pull back the neck of her robe please."

So that was why he'd called for the officer. Victoria should have known. He hadn't needed any help, and he wasn't going to let the female officer do the fingerprinting. He was insuring himself against any chance of a later accusation of impropriety. The thought made her ears burn. As if she'd stoop to lying.

"He turned her onto her stomach and wrapped both hands around her neck. Do I have that right, Ms. Kirkland?"

Victoria shuddered. His words brought back the terror, the helplessness, the dreadful certainty that she was going to die. Was he doing that on purpose? Taunting her? Forcing her to relive those awful seconds that she'd thought were her last?

She heard the sound of paper being peeled off its backing. She was expecting him to press the sticky film against her neck, but she still jumped when he did.

"Try to stand still," he said, his voice kinder than it had been so far, "and keep your hair out of the way."

He gently wrapped his fingers around the right side of her neck, pressing the paper firmly against her skin. Chills skittered down her spine. She stiffened. There was a vast difference between his firm hands and her attacker's thick, punishing fingers, yet the fear was still there.

He peeled the tape off, and after a couple of seconds he pressed a second strip onto the left side of her neck, against the worst bruise. She jerked away and bit off a gasp of pain.

The pressure eased immediately. "Sorry. It won't be much longer." He cradled the right side of her head in his right hand as he pressed the tape down with his left.

The warmth of his palm cradling her head sent a surprising tingle of awareness through her. She must be more rattled than she'd thought if she was reacting to this overbearing Texas Ranger who'd made it clear how much he detested her.

And she understood why. She'd believed in Gary Zelke's innocence or she wouldn't have given in to his plea to represent him. And although the expert she'd hired had found evidence the police had missed—evidence that proved another car had rammed Caroline's Corvette prior to Gary's—Brody McQuade still resented her.

He peeled the tape off her neck. "Okay. You can let your hair down."

She let go of her hair and massaged her cramped shoulder.

"Label those if you would," Brody said to Officer Martin. "Left side, right side. You know the drill. And take them upstairs to Sergeant Caldwell."

Victoria turned around and her kimono slipped down one arm. She grabbed it and pulled it back up, but not before Brody's dark, intense eyes zeroed in on her bare shoulder and nearly exposed breast.

She stared at him, daring him to look her in the eye.

He did.

"Why did you do that?" she asked.

His brows lowered and his gaze flickered briefly downward. "Do what?" he said harshly.

"Fingerprint my neck. Why didn't you have Officer Martin do it?" As antsy as she still was, she couldn't completely hide a smile at his reaction. Had he really thought she would ask why he'd looked at her nearly naked breast?

She did like the idea that he was enough of a guy to look. "Oh…"

Well, what do you know? He was cute when he was flustered. She'd seen him angry, cold, devastated by grief and disgusted. And she'd seen him calm, efficient and stiffly official. But although she'd noticed his even features, the cleft in his chin and his strong jaw, the word *cute* had never occurred to her in relation to him. She was pretty sure he wouldn't appreciate the description.

"I didn't want to depend on secondhand information. I wanted to see for myself."

Apprehension pooled at the base of her spine. "See what?"

He studied her for a moment, a small frown wrinkling his brow. He seemed to be trying to make up his mind about something.

Then he took a couple of steps backward, away from her, and looked at the floor. She was a good attorney, a good judge of people and an excellent reader of body language. He'd distanced himself from her because he was going to tell her something she didn't want to hear.

"There have been seven break-ins in the past eight months. Four occurred while the people weren't home." He walked over to the windows.

"Right. Everyone here has talked about how lucky they were."

"Were they?"

Brody was looking out over the Cantara Hills Golf Course. But she knew his eyes weren't on the spectacular view. He was turned inward, struggling with something.

"What are you saying?"

He didn't answer, nor did he move. He stood outlined by the darkness beyond the windows, his arms crossed and his feet planted shoulder-distance apart, his back at once strong-and vulnerable-looking in his white dress shirt.

She walked over and put herself between him and the window. "What are you saying?" she repeated.

He looked down at her. "Why do you think Zelke and Briggs and you were the only ones attacked?"

She shook her head. "That's what I asked you."

"Do you know what was stolen from each apartment?"

Victoria was having trouble following his logic. "Not much."

"That's right. *Not much.* The guy barely took enough to call it a burglary. And not one thing that can be traced. No custom jewelry, nothing large. Insignificant stuff."

"But he took an antique humidor from Byron Dalloway and about five thousand in cash from Mrs. Winger and a diamond-and-emerald bracelet from Jane Majorsky—"

"Insignificant."

She frowned. "But if burglary wasn't the motive, then…"

His intense gaze taunted her, dared her to say what she was thinking.

"You *do* think the break-ins were a cover. You think…"

"You three were the real targets. And if I'm right, he'll be back for you."

Chapter Two

Two hours later, back in the conference suite, their temporary headquarters at the Cantara Hills Country Club, Brody looked up from his laptop at the sound of plastic sliding against metal, and then the soft whirr of a computer-driven lock release. The hall door swung open. Egan came in, wiping a hand down his face.

"Where's the evidence?" Brody asked.

"It's in the car," Egan said on a yawn. "Could you give me time to get my tail in the door before you chew on it?"

Brody didn't bother to answer him. He finished typing in his impressions of the crime scene and Victoria Kirkland's condition.

Caucasian female, thirty years old, five foot nine inches— He stopped, picturing her standing in front of him with one shoulder of that black-and-red kimono sliding down her delicately muscled arm. She was slender but not skinny. He went back to typing—*130 pounds, blond hair, green eyes.*

"Hot and cool at the same time." Egan's voice came from behind him. "Like a hot fudge sundae."

Brody kicked his chair back and whirled in one motion.

"Whoa!" Egan backpedaled. Water flew in an arc across the tile floor as he fumbled with the plastic bottle he held.

"This is not a joke."

"Hey, I know that. But you've got to lighten up. I don't think you've slept a night through since…"

Since Kimberly's death. The unspoken words hung between them, echoing in Brody's head. His old life had ended and this new obsessed one had begun the night his sister died.

"I'm fine," he growled.

Egan took a step back. "No, you're not. Look, Brody. I respect what you're doing. God knows I've admired your abilities all my life, but you shouldn't be on this case. You're burning yourself out."

Brody sent him a glare and sat back down at the mahogany conference table. He stared at the laptop screen, but the words were a blur.

He heard the plastic water bottle hit the trash. "Do us both a favor and get your butt to bed. That report'll be there in the morning."

Brody wiped a hand across his face. When he did, the faint scent of roses drifted across his nostrils. He'd washed his hands. How did they still carry her scent? "Yeah, the report'll be here, but the perp will be back in his spider-hole. What have you got for evidence?"

"Damn little. Whoever did this is careful, but we already knew that from the other break-ins. There was nothing in the bedroom, but I've got the bedclothes."

"Nothing? No hairs? No fibers?"

Egan wiped his face. "Nope. Not that we saw. We picked up a few prints."

"What about how he got in?"

"It had to be the back door. We found prints on the back stairs."

"Back door? Back stairs?"

"Yeah. That is one big penthouse."

"I wish I'd known about the stairs."

Egan yawned. "I got it covered. I took fingerprints and got one good photo of a boot print in dust. Most of them were smudged."

"Good job." Brody closed the laptop and looked at his watch. "I want you up at seven. Get that evidence to Austin. We could have a partial print from Victoria's neck."

"Seven?" Egan checked his watch and groaned.

"You got a problem with that?"

Egan averted his gaze and shook his head. "Nope." He rubbed his eyes. "Two hours and forty-three minutes' worth of sleep. No problem."

"Where are the case files for Briggs and Zelke?"

"I haven't touched them. They're wherever you left them."

"I want the lab to compare fingerprints. I think I got a couple of good ones off Victoria's neck."

"*You?* You processed her?"

"The female cop was a rookie. I didn't want it messed up."

"I don't think they tried to take prints off Briggs's and Zelke's skin, and there were no usable prints in their apartments."

Brody cursed. "I don't guess it would do any good to exhume them."

"All right, Lieutenant. Now I'm sure you're losing it. They were washed and autopsied and embalmed. You've got to get some sleep."

"Yeah," Brody said on a sigh. "I guess I do."

Egan headed for his room.

Brody headed for his. At his door he turned back. "Caldwell."

Egan sighed and let his forehead fall against the door frame.

"Stay up there in Austin. I want to hear back on the lab's findings as soon as they happen."

"Let Hayes do it. He's already there. He can—"

"You were at the scene. I want you. Send Hayes back here. I've got a job for him, too."

"Yeah?"

Brody nodded. "I want him to chase down the items that were stolen from the apartments."

"I don't think Briggs or Zelke had anything stolen."

"I'm talking about the break-ins where nobody was home."

"What for? You said yourself nothing traceable was taken."

"The perp is smart. But what use has he got for an antique humidor or an emerald bracelet?"

Egan's mouth stretched in a yawn. "Maybe he smokes cigars. Maybe his girlfriend will get a real nice birthday present this year."

"I'm banking on him preferring money. If he pawned the stuff or sold it to an antique store, maybe we can trace it. And if we can trace it, we can trace him."

Egan rubbed his eyes. "Good point. What about you? What are you going to do?"

"I want every single entry card for Cantara Gardens accounted for. Victoria's penthouse card, the manager's master, the household staff. I especially want to know who's asked for a replacement card in the past eight months. And what they do with cards when tenants leave—or die."

"Makes sense. That's got to be how the perp gets in without setting off the alarm system."

"Somebody, either on purpose or accidentally, gave the murderer entry into Cantara Gardens, and I intend to find out who it is."

THE BRUISES WERE WORSE this morning. Victoria lifted her chin and touched the sore places with her fingers, watching her reflection in the downstairs-bathroom mirror.

Icy fear slid down her spine and nausea swirled in her gut as she recalled those hot, rough fingers cutting off her breath. She wrapped her arms protectively around her middle and rested her forehead against the cool mirror, waiting for the queasiness to pass.

She'd showered last night after the police and Brody had left, but this morning she still felt dirty—violated. And her pristine apartment had ceased to be a sanctuary. She'd slept on the sofa in the living room because she couldn't make herself get into the bed where the man had attacked her.

It didn't matter that Detective Sergeant Deason had stationed an officer in the elevator lobby. It wouldn't have mattered if the officer had been guarding her bedroom door. She didn't think she'd ever be able to sleep in that bed again.

The attacker would be back. Brody McQuade had said so last night, and she knew he was right.

A harsh jangling sent her heart into her throat.

Phone. It was just her phone. She took a deep breath and shook off the panic that had gripped her. Why hadn't she ever noticed how much the phone's ring sounded like her security alarm?

She picked up the handset on the third ring, glancing at the ornate clock perched on a shelf. Was it really only seven-thirty?

"Victoria, sweetheart."

It was Tammy Sutton, the wife of the powerful chairman of the San Antonio City Board. Victoria grimaced. She could tell by the tone of Tammy's voice that she already knew what had happened.

"Hi, Tammy," she said, forcing a brightness into her voice.

Of course Tammy would know about the break-in. Not even uber-Ranger Brody McQuade could stop the police from reporting the incident to Kenneth Sutton.

"I do apologize for calling so early, but I heard about your attack and I just had to see if you're all right. What on earth happened?"

"I'm not sure I should be talking about it."

"Nonsense. I'm your friend. You need someone to lean on right now."

Friend? Hardly. She and Tammy were on a couple of charity committees together. Victoria's grandmother would not have approved of the cavalier way people threw around the word friend these days. She'd have called them speaking acquaintances.

"That's very nice of you to offer—"

"Sweetheart. It's what friends are for." Butter wouldn't melt in Tammy's mouth, she thought. The woman was up to something. Victoria almost laughed at that thought. When was Tammy Sutton not up to something? The woman could chew up and spit out anybody, then rinse her mouth with a Long Island Iced Tea.

"Tell me what happened. Could you identify the attacker? Did he say anything?"

"No. It all happened so fast. And he didn't say a word. He just tried to choke me."

"Oh, my God! And you didn't see anything?"

"Not a thing." Victoria wasn't about to give Tammy the

details of how she'd come awake just as the man grabbed her and flipped her onto her stomach. The horror of what could have happened still chilled her to the bone.

"Oh, Victoria. Are you sure you're all right? He didn't—"

"I'm fine. Just a little shaken. Now I really have to get ready for work."

"Work? Victoria, what is the matter with you? You're in no shape to work. My God, you could have been killed."

Victoria's mouth tasted like ash. She could happily have gone all day without hearing that. She licked her lips and sucked in a breath. "Working will help. In fact, it will help a lot, since I've got stacks of paperwork to finish. For once I'll welcome the boredom. I'm fine, really."

She was so *not* fine, but she wasn't going to let anyone know that. She'd built her reputation as an attorney—face it, she'd built her life—on her ability to stay cool no matter what the situation.

She'd had trouble hanging on to her signature cool last night in the presence of Brody McQuade, and that dismayed her.

She didn't like the sense of safety she'd felt from the moment he'd walked into the room. She didn't like the sexual attraction that had sparked between them in an arc of electricity that she'd have sworn was visible.

Most of all, she didn't like Brody's air of supreme confidence. He knew he was in charge and his confidence was palpable to anyone he came in contact with.

She'd dealt with guys like him, guys who used bullying to get their way. For some inexplicable reason, she was drawn to the caveman type, but at least she'd learned to recognize them and avoid them.

"Hello? Victoria?"

"Oh, sorry, Tammy. I…I thought I heard something."

"See? You're obviously too upset to work. Why don't you spend a few days at my lake house? It's got all the comforts— even the freezer's stocked."

"Thank you, but I can't leave in the middle of this investigation."

Tammy Sutton had always been gracious at dinners and teas, but she'd never made overtures to Victoria. Until today. Victoria couldn't help but wonder what Tammy's motive was.

A faint beep sounded in Victoria's ears. "Tammy, I have another call. It could be the police."

"Oh, of course. I'll let you go. We must get together for lunch soon."

"That would be lovely. Bye." *I won't hold my breath until I hear from you.*

She picked up the incoming call. "Hello?"

"Victoria, are you all right?" It was Caroline Stallings.

"What's going on, Caroline? How does everybody know about my attack?"

"It's on the early-morning news. They didn't say much about your condition, so I had to call. I'm so glad you're not in the hospital."

"How do they do it? The media, I mean. I didn't see a reporter anywhere."

"Tell me about it. I often get the idea that certain people would be happy to have every move they made played out on television. So they delight in talking to the press about anything."

"Well, I've had about enough of this latest media circus. I'm seriously considering moving."

"I know. This whole year has been so bizarre. Do you

realize that three people we know have died in the past eight months?"

"Three? Oh—you mean starting with Kimberly."

Caroline paused infinitesimally. "Yes, and all three were such tragedies."

An eerie chill spread through Victoria. "Sometimes I wonder—"

"If there's a connection? Me, too."

Victoria heard her sigh. "Caroline, Kimberly's death wasn't your fault."

"I was driving, and Kimberly didn't have her seat belt on. There are two people who are certain it was my fault. Lieutenant Brody McQuade and me."

"It was tragic, but it certainly wasn't your fault. The only person at fault was the driver who ran away from the scene."

"I'm the only one who can say what happened, and I have no idea," Caroline said. "Until I can remember what happened…"

"Still nothing?"

"Zero. Zilch. *Nada*. I'd always heard about amnesia, but I guess I never really believed someone could actually have zero memory of something that happened to them. And yet here I am, living proof."

Victoria heard the chimes of her intercom. "Now there's someone at the door. Looks like I'm the most popular person in Cantara Hills this morning." She'd tried to make her voice light, but knew she'd failed.

"Don't let them get you down. Are you going to work?"

"Planning to. I'm sure not staying here all day."

The chimes rang again. "I'd better go. It might be Lieutenant McQuade, wanting to harass me some more." Her words were sarcastic, but deep inside, Victoria felt a twinge of anticipation.

What the heck was wrong with her? Did she actually want to see Brody again? Want to experience that sense of safety and power again? Last night he'd filled her apartment with his comforting presence.

"Victoria, if you need to talk or if you just want to get a drink or have lunch or something, let me know."

Victoria thanked her and hung up. She looked down at herself. She was still in the ivory gown and black-and-red kimono. She started toward the intercom, reaching to turn on the security camera's monitor.

But before she got to it a *ping* announced the arrival of the elevators. She recoiled.

Who…? Nobody but the manager had a master access card capable of sending the elevator to the penthouse. She clutched her kimono together at the neck and waited, paralyzed with fear, as the doors slid open.

Chapter Three

It was him. Brody McQuade. He stepped into her foyer looking like a poster for the Texas Rangers in dress khakis, a crisp white shirt, shiny badge on his chest and the signature fawn-colored Stetson held in his left hand. The only thing missing was a tooled-leather holster.

She met his gaze and saw that he was eyeing her clothing just like she'd eyed his.

His brows rose. "Morning, Ms. Kirkland. I didn't mean to get you out of bed."

Victoria's hand tightened at her neck. "How…what…how did you get up here?"

He held up a plastic card. "Master. From the manager." Was that a twinkle in his eye? It couldn't have been. Brody's dark eyes weren't the twinkling kind.

"Mark Patterson is not supposed to give *anyone* access to the penthouse."

Brody didn't comment.

She narrowed her gaze suspiciously. "I wasn't in bed. I'm being deluged with phone calls. Apparently everyone in San Antonio knows about last night."

"Deluged?"

Dear heavens, it *was* a twinkle. Victoria felt her chest tighten in anger. He thought she was *funny?*

She propped her fists on her hips, then noticed what that did to her kimono. So she wrapped it around her again and crossed her arms tightly. "Two people have called already and now you're here."

"I see what you mean by deluged."

He nodded solemnly, but Victoria knew sarcasm when she heard it. She ignored it. "I thought the media had to have permission to use victims' names."

"You're the attorney. You ought to know."

"What can I do for you, Lieutenant?"

"I'm canvassing the tenants about their access cards. Whoever attacked you must have had a card, because there was no unauthorized access. No breach of the system, either."

"Well, that should be easy. Who used their cards last night?"

"I'm waiting for the manager to get me a printout."

"So you want to see my card?"

"Thought I'd start at the top."

"Could you give me a minute to dress?"

His gaze flickered. "Yes, ma'am. I'll go back down to the lobby and wait."

"Come inside, Lieutenant. There's no reason for you to wait downstairs." She excused herself and went upstairs for the first time since the police had left the night before. Her bedroom was still a wreck from the CSIs.

Victoria dressed quickly, averting her eyes from the stripped bed, the misarranged furniture and the fine film of fingerprint dust that covered every surface.

When she came back down, Brody wasn't in the foyer and the elevator doors were closed. Had he left? Gone down to the lobby to wait, after all?

"Lieutenant?" she called, suddenly nervous. The penthouse was huge, ridiculously large for one person. For the first time since she'd moved in she felt small and vulnerable. "Lieutenant? Brody?"

"In here."

The kitchen. She followed his voice across the quarry tile to the open door that led into her walk-in pantry, laundry room and trash bin. Brody was examining the door to the hallway.

"I wanted to see where the perp got in."

"That's the fire-escape door. The stairs are just to the left."

"And your penthouse card works in this door, too. My master does."

"Yes."

"Who comes in this way?"

"No one."

"How do you handle trash, recycling, laundry?"

"I set the trash and the recycling out this door and Maintenance picks it up. I do my own laundry."

"Where do the stairs go?"

"All the way down to the basement, I think. But Maintenance takes the elevator to the third floor, then walks up the fire stairs. They never come inside."

"Maintenance doesn't have a card for the penthouse?"

"No. That's why I put my trash out myself."

He gave her a hard look, then went back to studying the door. "There's no sign of forced entry. The perp had to have a master card or one that accesses the penthouse."

"I have never given anyone a card," she said sharply.

Brody took a pen-size flashlight out of his pocket and examined the door. "What about these dead bolts? They look like the original locks."

"They are. These condos were built in the late seventies. That's why there's a guardhouse. The guard would operate the gate to let the tenants in."

"Do you have a key to the dead bolt?"

"Yes, but I think I'm the only one."

"The only one. Why's that?"

"Well, other than the staff. I've never paid much attention. But it seems like I've heard the housekeepers rattling keys."

"So if the staff have a key, how can you be sure they don't come in?"

"They'd have to use the card and the key to get into the penthouse. This is the only apartment that requires an electronic card to get in."

"What about the other tenants? Zelke, Briggs?"

Victoria shook her head. "Their cards are for the gate and the lobby door. Oh, and their keys didn't fit each other's locks."

"How do you know that?"

"They told me. Because they were guys, they tried the keys."

Brody pushed his fingers through his hair in frustration. "Somebody dropped the ball on the keys. The manager should have told me about them, or the homeowners' association. *Some*body I've talked to had to have known about the keys. Either they're too dumb to know how important those keys are, or they're protecting someone."

As he spoke, Victoria remembered playing with a ring of keys on the floor of her grandfather's house.

I built you the biggest house in the world, Toto, and when you grow up, you'll live there like a princess in an ivory tower.

Thinking about her grandfather made her sad. Thinking about the *ivory tower* made her shiver.

She took a deep breath. "Well, the answer is 'too dumb to know how important they are.'"

"What are you talking about?"

"It's me. I know about the keys. Until you asked about them I hadn't thought about them in years."

"Years? What are you talking about?"

Victoria nodded. "My grandpa designed and built Cantara Gardens."

"Your grandfather?" Brody's tone dripped with exasperation. "Why didn't you tell me?"

"Because I didn't think about it. That was more than twenty-five years ago. I was in preschool, or grade school."

She knew she sounded defensive. She *was*. This…*Ranger,* with his hot intensity and unbending attitude, expected everyone to be as single-minded and passionate as he was. Not that she could blame him. His little sister, his only family, was dead, and the killer lived somewhere in Cantara Hills.

"So your grandfather owns the condos? I guess it's easy to see how you could forget that your grandfather is probably the one person who could tell us who has keys. Please tell me he's alive."

"Oh, don't worry. Lucky for you he's still around."

Brody winced. "I didn't mean it like that. It's just—"

"I know how you meant it." She angled her head and sent him a disgusted look. "No, Grandpa doesn't own the condos. He was a contractor. But his contract with the homeowners' association contained one caveat. That the penthouse at Cantara Gardens would always be available for use by the Kirklands."

Brody's expression deteriorated into disgust. "So you don't even pay for this massive waste of electricity and resources?"

Victoria stuck her chin in the air. "That's right, Lieutenant

McQuade. I don't even pay for it. I wonder how long it's going to take you to get over the money thing. I wouldn't have thought you were such a snob."

Brody gaped at her. "Snob?" He took a long breath. "I'm not a snob and I don't give a damn about whose money is whose. I just want to find out who killed Kimmie." He hadn't meant to say that. He'd meant to say *who was killing tenants in the condos.*

Her eyes, which had been sparking with anger, turned soft. "Oh, poor Kimberly. Brody, I am so sorry—I haven't even asked how you're doing."

He held up a hand. "Save it. You said enough at the time."

He looked at the keyhole in the back door, shining the little flashlight this way and that, trying to see if he could detect any metal flakes. He pulled out his cell phone and called Egan.

"Working hard, boss," Egan said as soon as he answered.

"Caldwell, did you check the dead bolt on the back door of Victoria's penthouse? Had a key been used?"

"I swabbed the keyhole. It looked like there might be some metal shavings. I've got the swab."

"Good. The shavings looked new?"

"I'll have to get them under the microscope, but I think so."

"Thanks." Brody pocketed his phone and turned to Victoria. "Where's your grandfather now?"

"He's in a nursing home near my parents' home."

Nursing home. His heart sank. "Is he lucid?"

Victoria's lips curled up in a little smile. "Oh, yes, indeed. He can still beat me at chess."

"So what's he doing in a nursing home?"

"He's diabetic, and he had a massive stroke several years ago. He's paralyzed on his right side. He needs constant care."

"Where are your parents?"

She cocked her head. "You mean you don't know?"

"I know where they live. I know they're retired and they spend a lot of time traveling. But no, I don't know exactly where they are."

"Let's see. This is August? Then they're on a photo-safari in Kenya."

"Can we talk to your grandfather? I'd like to be able to account for all of the old keys."

"I don't know. He's a proud man. I'm not sure he'd want a Lieutenant Texas Ranger to see him so helpless and weak."

Brody understood, but this wasn't about an old man's dignity or about respecting the elderly. This was about Kimmie.

It was a cinch, though, that Victoria was going to be protective of her grandfather. He'd ask the manager, but unless the manager could account for every single master key, he'd have to insist on seeing Victoria's grandfather.

"At least now I've got a pretty good idea how the perp got into the other apartments. Somehow, he has a card that lets him in through the front gate and the lobby door, and then he used a master key to let himself into the apartments."

He closed the back door. "But the penthouse is different. None of the other apartments have two levels. None have a set of back stairs. And none of the other apartments require the use of a master electronic card."

He looked around the small space. There was a second door between the clothes dryer and the wall. "I guess that's the door to the back stairwell?"

Brody opened the door, which meant he had to step backward. His arm pressed against her breast.

She pulled away and her back hit the wall.

Working hard at ignoring the feel of her breast against his arm, he shone his flashlight up the dark stairwell. "So the perp managed to get in the back door, and he came up the back stairs. That's how he got to you before your alarm sounded. He only had a fifteen-second window, right?"

She nodded.

"Caldwell processed the stairwell. He said he found a good bootprint in the dust. Do you not use these stairs?"

Victoria looked up at the narrow spiral staircase. "I don't like them. It's awfully cramped in there, and kind of spooky because it's so steep."

"What about your housekeeper?"

Her hackles rose. Why did everything he said make her defensive? "I don't have a housekeeper. So nobody uses it."

He looked up at her, his dark gaze mesmerizing. "Tell me exactly how long it's been since these stairs have been used."

"I moved in here two years ago last December. When I looked at the apartment the manager insisted on taking me all over, including up the stairs." She gave a small, dry chuckle. "I think he just wanted to watch me walk up the stairs in a straight skirt."

Brody's brain immediately conjured up an eight-by-ten glossy of the manager's view from the bottom of the stairs. He clenched his jaw. "So you've *never* used the stairs since?"

She looked him in the eye and lifted her chin. "Okay, in the interest of full disclosure—"

Ah, hell. She was about to spout lawyer crap for who knew how long, and when she was done he wouldn't know any more than he already did.

"The week I moved in, I had an open house. There were probably fifty people or more. Everyone was touring the place."

"So there could have been fifty people on these stairs? Fifty people who saw your back door with the dead bolt, and who know the back stairs lead right up to the hall outside your bedroom."

She hadn't thought about that. He could see it in her eyes. "It…it was just a party."

He sighed. "Tell me who was here, if you can remember."

"I have the list. I had a guest book, and afterward, I put the names into a database."

Brody stared. "A database?"

She shrugged and her cheeks turned pink. "For holiday cards."

"Okay. Who?"

"Gary Zelke, Miles Landis—he's Taylor Landis's brother—Tammy and Kenneth Sutton, actually the whole homeowners' association dropped by."

"Link Hathaway?"

"Yes, and his daughter, Margaret."

"What about Briggs?"

"He hadn't moved in yet."

"And I don't guess Carlson was there."

"No, thank goodness. But Jane Majorsky was."

"The woman whose bracelet was stolen? What about the others—Dalloway or Amanda Winger?"

"I don't remember. I'll get you the database."

"So that's it? One party two and a half years ago?" He wasn't sure he believed her. "No more parties?"

Clouds gathered in her green eyes. "I'm not much of a party person."

"Yeah? So if you've never had another party, what about your holiday-card list? They come around to visit you one at a time?"

"Are you saying that one of them did this?" Her words may have sounded indignant, but her voice didn't. She knew it was true. She just didn't want to know.

"It's likely that one of them hired someone—I'm sure most of the people on your list couldn't or wouldn't kill someone with their bare hands. But if I could narrow the suspect list to fifty people, I'd be happy."

She looked like she'd happily rip her tongue out if it meant she didn't have to answer any more questions. "There aren't fifty people anymore."

Now he was getting somewhere. He wasn't sure where. "Right. Zelke is dead."

Her gaze wavered. "Yes, and…"

"And?"

"Well, my ex."

Her ex? Ex-what? he wondered, and stopped his thoughts right there. It didn't matter. "He's not in the picture any longer?"

She paused, not looking at him. The tiny laundry room seemed to shrink as Brody tried to maintain his detachment. It shouldn't make a bit of difference to him whether she was in a relationship or not.

"No."

The word was curt.

Brody started to ask where the guy was, when suddenly Victoria stiffened and a hand flew to her mouth.

"Dear heavens, that's it!"

Brody's pulse jumped. "What's it?" He reached for her. "Are you okay?"

"Sorry, I'm fine. I just remembered something. He was wearing cologne. Expensive cologne." Her face was transformed. "I should have recognized it right away. It's called

Torture. It's a top brand in Europe. My ex used it. I think because he liked the name."

Brody frowned. "You're saying the perp smelled like this expensive cologne? So what kind of *expensive* are we talking about? Expensive as in *I'm worth it* or expensive as in *if you have to ask?*"

If Victoria Kirkland thought it was expensive, it must be made from unicorn blood or something.

Her mouth quirked up. "Expensive as in *nobody's* worth that. It's over two hundred dollars an ounce for the cologne. I bought my ex a bottle one Christmas."

"So I guess *he* was worth it."

"Like I said, nobody's worth that."

Brody took a small notebook out of his jacket pocket and jotted down the name of the cologne. Beside it he made a note to check with the other break-in victims to see if they remembered the scent. It was a long shot. The scent could easily have faded before the victims got home. The only two who could verify that the perp was wearing expensive cologne were dead.

"So what kind of ex was he? Husband?"

That question was totally irrelevant and Victoria's face told Brody she knew it. So he tried to make it relevant. "Could it have been your ex who attacked you? Maybe he still has a key?"

The storm clouds were back in her eyes. "What kind of question is that? There have been seven break-ins—eight now. Two of my friends have been killed. And you're trying to turn this into a lovers' spat? I can assure you it wasn't my ex-fiancé."

"What's his name?"

"It wasn't him." Her voice was harsh.

Brody met her gaze.

To her credit and his surprise she didn't flinch. She lifted her chin. "Rayburn Andrews."

Brody's eyebrows shot up. "The heir to the cosmetics fortune? I thought he died."

Victoria's eyes closed briefly. "He went down in his private plane on a trip to Cancun."

"Sorry," he said automatically. Her words conjured up unwelcome memories of his parents. Was her ex a jet-setting thrill-seeker like they were? Was *she?*

"So we've got a perp who can get past security alarms and into a secure penthouse, and who wears super-expensive cologne."

He thought about his long list of suspects. "Who else do you know who wears—" he glanced at his notepad "—Torture?"

"Unfortunately, I've noticed it a lot of places. It's become ridiculously popular, probably because it's so expensive."

Brody raised his brows.

"It's a distinctive scent, but it smells horrible if someone uses too much. I've noticed it, but I'm not sure I can say for sure on who. I really don't pay attention."

"Well, if you notice anybody, tell me." He glanced around the spacious penthouse. "You need to beef up your personal-security system, have them take that damn fifteen-second delay off the alarm."

"So you really think he'll try again?"

"He's extremely organized—one break-in a month, one fatality every third month. You threw a wrench into the works—upset his schedule. We have no idea what he's going to do next. But I want you prepared."

Her gaze met his. "You think you know who it is, don't you?"

Brody shook his head. "No. Not yet. But I think the man who killed Briggs and Zelke and who tried to kill you is one of your neighbors."

Chapter Four

The sound of a card triggering the door lock didn't surprise Brody. He'd been expecting Hayes Keller, the third Ranger working with him on the Cantara Gardens murders. He finished writing the last name on the whiteboard as the door opened.

"So where have you been?" he asked, glancing at his watch. It was after ten.

"Drinking beer and watching strippers."

Brody shot Hayes one of his patented silencer looks.

"Hey—" Hayes tossed his Stetson onto a chair and held up his hands, palms out "—I was finishing up a case. *Twenty-four/seven, we never sleep*. That's our motto, right?"

Brody allowed himself a tiny smile. It was an old joke. "Nope. The Ranger motto is *One riot, one Ranger*."

"That, too." Hayes stepped over to the whiteboard. "What's all this?"

"The printout on the table lists every tenant of Cantara Gardens who used their access cards on the night of Victoria's attack." Brody pointed toward two thin manila folders. "Those are Briggs's and Zelke's case files with printouts of card use on the night each died. I'm comparing the lists."

Hayes looked at the board. "Lotta names." He pointed. "Do all these show up on all three nights? Damn busy place, those condos."

"Tell me about it. I spent all day today talking to the tenants. There are forty units. All are occupied. Fifty-two tenants total. The manager's records list seventy-eight active cards."

"Whoa! So I take it the manager isn't too careful about controlling card access. You got the breakdown of who's where?"

"Twenty-nine are singles. Eleven couples, and one couple has her mother living with them. Twenty-nine plus twenty-three accounts for the fifty-two official tenants. Who knows how many of the singles have live-in friends."

Hayes looked at the board. "He's got seventy-eight active cards for fifty-two tenants? That's twenty-six cards unaccounted for. You think there are that many freeloaders?"

Brody shook his head. "I'm hoping most of the cards are lost or destroyed, but there's no record. The manager apparently gave 'em out like Halloween candy. I don't think the man ever saw a request for a card he didn't grant."

"What are you going to do?"

"I'm calling a special meeting of the Cantara Hills Homeowners' Association to talk about changing out the condos' security system. If I had my way, I'd change out the manager, too. I've got an SAPD officer meeting with each tenant to round up duplicate cards. That'll narrow the field a little bit." Brody arched his neck and massaged the tight tendons of his shoulders.

Hayes yawned and headed for the kitchen. "Want a beer?"

"Nah. Just water." Brody stared at the grid he'd drawn on the whiteboard. He had three columns, headed *Briggs, Zelke* and *Victoria*. Under each he'd listed every card access recorded by the security-system computer from noon until 2:00 a.m. starting on the date of each attack.

He rubbed a hand over his face and sat down. All the numbers were beginning to run together.

Hayes tossed him a bottle of water and sat on the other side of the table. Brody turned up the bottle and drank half of it in one gulp.

"That's a lot of people coming and going," Hayes said, echoing the remark he'd made earlier.

"Look at the repeats." Some names had shown up on the entry log several times during one evening.

"Does the system show exits?"

"I wish. Just entries through the gate."

"So Jane Majorsky, for instance, who came in three times on the day Briggs was killed and once on Zelke's day, and twice the day Victoria was attacked, might have loaned her card to someone else."

Brody nodded again and then finished his water. "She could have loaned her card or she could have given somebody her original card and gotten a duplicate from the manager. There's nothing that indicates when the card was made."

"Pretty sloppy."

"And dangerous."

"So how many of those cards did you personally see?"

Brody dug his small notebook out of his pants pocket and flipped pages. He quickly counted the list of names he'd jotted down as he talked to tenants. "I've got thirty-four names. And there were twelve apartments where I got no answer."

"It's late and I never was good at the fox, geese and grain game. Figured out anything from all this?"

Brody leaned back in his chair, balancing it on the two back legs. He gestured with his empty water bottle. "Amanda Winger used her entry card three times on the night of Briggs's murder, once on Zelke's night and twice last night. And get this. Ms. Winger is seventy-eight."

"What's she doing in a ritzy swinging-singles' condo?"

"Actually, she's a special case. She's Tammy Sutton's mother, and of course Kenneth Sutton is head of the board."

"So Tammy Sutton probably has a card that reads Amanda Winger."

"Kenneth Sutton could, too. There's no telling."

"What about Miles Landis? His name is on there."

"Yep. His card was used twice each night. Between six-thirty and seven-thirty, then again later. Close to midnight."

Brody stood and checked off their names.

"There's no difference in the cards? Date issued? One says duplicate?"

Brody shook his head tiredly. "There's nothing on the card except the tenant's name and apartment number. And get this, the housekeeping and maintenance staff all use the same coded card. That one just says *staff*. The only place their cards don't work is on the penthouse. *And* if that's not enough, the staff also have master keys to the dead bolts, so they can get in to clean. Biggest mess I've ever seen. I'm recommending to the board that they find themselves a new manager."

"Security cameras?"

"I've already been through all that. There's no guard in the guardhouse to check ID and no camera on the gate.

"The only security camera in the whole place is the one in front of the elevators in Victoria Kirkland's suite. Egan has the disk, but Deason's right. We're not going to see anything. Whoever attacked her didn't come through the front entrance."

"So what about Victoria Kirkland? Egan said she wasn't injured. Did she see anything?"

Brody shook his head. "The perp attacked her from behind. She has bruises on her neck that are consistent with Zelke's and Briggs's injuries. I took fingerprints, but of course prints on skin are always a long shot."

"She's on all three lists."

Brody nodded. "She's obviously super-organized and efficient. She gets in within two minutes either side of six o'clock every day."

"Sounds more like super-anal. Any way she could have faked her injuries?"

Brody glowered at him.

"Hey—what? Did I step on toes?"

Brody ignored him. "Byron Dalloway has three entries last night, but none on the night of Zelke's murders and only one for the night of Briggs's murder."

Hayes stood and stretched. "So you're targeting the odd patterns, like the old lady going out three times in one night, and like Majorsky there. She's done a lot of coming and going."

"I'm working on the theory that whoever is doing this is using a duplicate card they got from one of the tenants. And has somehow obtained a master key to the dead bolts. The individual apartment keys are different."

Hayes started unbuttoning his shirt. "You don't think it's somebody who lives there?"

"I've got to start somewhere, and as flimsy as it is, the duplicate-card theory is the simplest. If it's someone who lives there…"

"We're screwed. Fifty-two suspects and no leads. I'm exhausted just thinking about it. I gotta take a shower and hit the hay."

VICTORIA SHIFTED POSITION on the sofa and tucked the afghan around her toes. She couldn't sleep—again. This was the second night she'd stayed downstairs. The idea of spending the night up in her bedroom with no way to escape if someone came after her sent fear skittering up and down her spine.

She stared up at the stars shining through the skylight. She'd get over it—eventually. But right now she was happy here, only twenty feet or so from her front door, with her cell phone tucked into the pocket of her silk pajamas. And a policeman was guarding the front lobby of the building again tonight.

She pulled the afghan up to her chin and closed her eyes, but her brain was wired and her muscles were cramped with tension. She tried to use relaxation techniques she'd learned in yoga to calm her mind and her body.

I relax my toes, my feet and my ankles. The relaxation spreads to my calves, my knees, and the muscles behind each knee. My feet and legs are completely relaxed.

The monotonous recitation began to loosen her tense muscles. *I relax my thighs, hips and tummy.* Maybe she could sleep, after all.

She took in a deep breath, using her breathing to help her relax.

A faint noise startled her. She froze. Had she really heard something, or was it her imagination? Holding her breath, her muscles tightening in the innate fight-or-flight response, she listened.

A creak sent her heart jumping into her throat. That was not her imagination. It was the door to the back stairs.

It was him. The killer. Her ears buzzed with panic. Her throat closed up. She couldn't swallow, couldn't speak.

Help me! She scissored her legs, kicking the afghan away.

The awful sensation of being overpowered and choked passed over her. Was it her imagination or could she hear his stealthy footsteps on the back stairs? Any second now he'd realize she wasn't in her bed.

She had to get out of here. Easing off the sofa, she moved quickly and silently to the entryway, sure she felt the killer's hot breath on the back of her neck.

She retrieved her cell phone from her pocket as she punched the call button for the elevator. Three stories below, she heard it rumble. Above her head, she heard a growled curse. He'd heard the elevator—or he'd found her bed empty.

A scream pushed against her tight throat. She pressed her knuckles against her mouth to stop it. Then she heard heavy footsteps headed toward the marble staircase.

He no longer cared about being quiet. He was stomping downstairs. He was coming after her!

She turned her back to the elevator and watched the stairs. What would she do if the elevator didn't come? She had absolutely nothing to use as a weapon.

She looked around the entryway. A large vase, a carved wooden box and a scented oil candle in a crystal bottle sat on an ornate table next to the elevator doors.

A vaudevillian image of a comic actor slipping on a banana peel flashed in her mind. She grabbed the bottle and threw it at the bottom stair. The musical crash of crystal shattering mingled with the *ping* of the bell as the elevator doors opened.

She heard his heavy steps on the marble. A shadow darkened the night-light that burned at the top of the stairs.

She hurled herself into the elevator and hit the button for the lobby. Then she jabbed at the close-door button until the doors slid shut. As the car began to move, she desperately tried to punch in the newest number in her phone—Brody McQuade's.

BRODY KNEW IT WAS Victoria before he completely woke up. He grabbed his phone.

"What's wrong?" He vaulted out of bed and reached for the nearest piece of clothing—his lightweight sweatpants.

"Help me! He's here." Her voice was raspy with panic.

"Get out. Not the back stairs! Not the elevator. Take the fire stairs!"

"I'm on the elevator," she panted.

"There's a cop in the lobby. Stay with him. I'll be right there." He pulled on the sweatpants and stuck his feet into running shoes and quickly tied them. Then he grabbed his gun and his phone.

He'd already decided that the four minutes it took to drive to the condos was three and a half minutes too long. So he pushed open the French doors that led from his sitting room out to the pool area. He hurdled the squat fence that surrounded the pool and broke into a run. Luckily there was a moon.

Arms pumping, chest heaving, legs pounding, he made it to the gates of Cantara Gardens in about forty seconds. He vaulted over the gate without breaking stride and took a quick glance around the grounds. Nothing seemed wrong. He grabbed his cell and dialed Hayes.

"Get up. Call Deason for backup. Here at the condos. Tell patrol cars in the area to get to the gate and not let any cars out."

"Wha—Brody?"

"Move it, Hayes. Do it! The killer's back."

"Gotcha." Hayes hung up.

Brody reached for the door to the lobby. Locked. He banged on the wood panels with the handle of his gun as he dug for the master access card. His fingers closed around it.

Before he got it inserted into the lock, the doorknob turned. He immediately went into weapon stance, holding the gun with two hands, but it was Victoria.

She dove straight into his arms. Her body shivered from head to toe. He wrapped her in his embrace for a few precious seconds. He wanted to hold her and tell her she was safe, but there was no time. And it would be a lie. Until he caught this guy, she'd never be safe.

He set her gently away and surveyed the lobby. The elevator she'd ridden in was standing open, as was the second car. The slick young MBA-type who managed the condos stood looking terror-stricken in silk pajamas with his spiked hair sticking out in all the wrong directions. "What's going on, Lieutenant? Do you think it's the same guy?"

"Where's the officer?"

"He, uh, he's checking the back stairs."

"Did you see him? Hear him?" he asked Victoria, ignoring the manager.

She shook her head, too fast. Too hard. "Heard him," she croaked.

"Take her inside," he instructed the manager. "I'm going to check on the officer."

"No!" Victoria cried. "Not alone."

"Go inside." He shot her a no-nonsense look as he pushed open the fire door.

The stairs were steep and the naked bulbs put out little more than night-lights. Another thing to mention to the homeowners' association. He focused his full attention on the stairs above his head. He moved slowly, his weapon trained on the last two steps he could see before they curved. His running shoes made no noise.

Where was the officer? A heavy dread settled in his chest. He stopped, listening. *Nothing.* He calculated the amount of time it had taken him to get here. Probably forty or fifty seconds, once he was out the door. Maybe a minute and a half total. Time enough for the perp to get down the stairs and out? Almost certainly. Time enough for him to kill the officer? He sure as hell hoped not.

The door from the lobby opened. Brody swung around, aiming at the door. It was one of the officers who'd assisted the other night.

"How many with you?" he whispered.

The officer held up four fingers.

"Check the stairs. I haven't found the officer stationed here tonight. He may be up there. Don't let anyone leave. I'm going down."

"Yes, sir."

The fire stairs didn't end at the first floor. They went down to the basement. Brody descended carefully, checking each step with his flashlight. This set of stairs was darker than the ones above, but the flashlight's beam showed wet footprints. His pulse leaped.

Evidence.

As he stepped off the bottom stair, he tripped over something and almost hit the ground. Hanging on to his balance, he swept his weapon around him, listening for the slightest noise. Nothing.

In the distance he heard police sirens. *Good.* Maybe they'd caught the killer. He felt along the wall for a switch and flipped on the light. Two five-gallon gas cans had been left at the foot of the stairs. There was no way anyone could see the green plastic containers in the darkness—no way to miss stepping on them.

The bastard had some sense.

Brody crossed to the door, leading with his flashlight beam, avoiding the prints.

He pushed the panic bar on the door with his forearm and swung his weapon as the door opened. The rear of the condos was one floor level below the front. The perp had known this. Did the fact that he'd escaped through the basement rather than heading back to his own apartment prove that he wasn't one of the residents?

Fresh footprints crushed the clover. By the light of the moon he followed them around to the side of the building and up the small hill. He could tell the guy had slipped on the wet grass on the hill.

The blue lights of the police cars lit up the sky. Steering clear of the prints, Brody climbed up to the parking-lot level. If the footprints belonged to the attacker, the guy was gone.

After finding out that neither Deason nor his men saw a vehicle leaving Cantara Gardens, Brody asked Deason to put out an APB for the area for any vehicles, and to sweep the grounds of the condos. Then he walked back into the lobby. Hayes was there talking to the manager, and two officers were stopping tenants at the elevator doors and sending them back up to their apartments with a curt explanation.

"Where's Vic?"

The manager and Hayes both looked at him questioningly.

"Vic?" Hayes parroted.

"Where is Victoria?"

The manager nodded toward his door. "She's in my kitchen. I think she made herself some tea."

"Hayes, thanks for taking care of stopping the tenants. Get

a couple of officers to canvass them. I want to know what each and every one of them was doing at the time of the attack."

Hayes nodded.

"And he left through the basement. Process the stairs yourself. Photos, impressions, the works."

"I'll take care of it, Lieutenant."

Brody stalked through the manager's living room into the kitchen. Victoria had her back to him. She was wearing a man's purple silk robe with pale blue piping. It hung almost to the ground. She'd folded the sleeves back. She finished pouring hot water over a teabag and then turned around.

"Oh!" Her hand went to her chest as her wide eyes lit on his weapon. "I didn't hear you. Is he gone?"

He immediately saw why the manager had given her a robe. All she had on under it were slinky satin pajamas.

"He's gone—or back in his apartment."

Her throat worked as she swallowed. "Do you really think he lives here?"

"Right now, anything's possible." He loosened his grip on his weapon for the first time and holstered it.

She nodded, then ducked her head and turned her back to him. "Do you want some tea?"

"No!"

Victoria flinched at his tone and almost spilled hot tea on her hands. Apparently she was never going to be able to successfully drink a cup of tea around Brody McQuade.

"I want to know what happened. How did he get into your place past your fancy alarm system?"

She took a shaky breath. "You told me to get it upgraded and to—how did you put it?—*get rid of that damned fifteen-second delay.*"

His brows drew down. "Yeah?"

"So I called first thing this morning. They came out this afternoon, took the system down, then realized a part was missing."

"You've got to be… Why didn't you tell me?" he shouted.

"Because I didn't *know* until late."

"Then you should have notified me late." His voice was icy.

She was bewildered by the way he treated her. He barked at her, glowered at her, and in general acted like he couldn't stand her.

That part was no mystery. She'd blown his case against Gary Zelke, the man who had been accused of killing his sister.

The part she didn't get was the other side of him. Whenever he touched her, it was with such tenderness it made her want to cry.

Right now he was eyeing her with a mixture of pensiveness and skepticism, obviously trying to decide what to do with her.

"All right, then. That settles it. Get some clothes together. You're coming with me."

"Where?" she asked apprehensively.

His eyes were hooded. His determination was apparent in the tic of his jaw muscle.

"I'm going to put you in a suite at the country club. Close to me. And you're going to stay close until we catch this serial killer."

Close to him? Victoria shook her head. "No."

No, no, no. That couldn't happen. "You don't have to do that. I can go to a hotel. I'll be safe there."

Brody's black eyes snapped with irritation.

"Don't you get it yet? You're not safe anywhere."

Chapter Five

Damn Brody McQuade and his broad shoulders and black eyes and those biceps. Victoria stretched and turned over in the bed, but it was no use.

She gave up and opened her eyes. The sun shone in a narrow stripe around the heavy draperies in the suite where Brody had stuck her at two o'clock this morning. Throwing back the covers, she got up, uttering a small groan when her stiff muscles protested. The suites at the Cantara Hills Country Club were huge and opulent, but the king-size bed wasn't comfortable. It was much too soft.

She felt like she hadn't slept a wink all night. Of course the dreams hadn't helped. Last night she'd been too scared to notice anything except Brody's comforting embrace, and then his undisguised irritation at her.

But obviously her subconscious mind had noticed a whole lot more, because as soon as he'd deposited her in this suite and she'd showered and climbed into bed, she'd been flooded with very sharp, very specific memories.

Memories of her first glimpse of Brody before she'd thrown herself into his arms. His face had been creased with worry, his bare arms corded with tension. Sweat had dampened his brown hair. He must have run all the way from the country club.

Then he'd pulled her into his hot embrace and pressed his cheek against hers. *It's okay. It's okay. I'm here now.*

Now *that* was a dream. Because Brody McQuade didn't say things like that—at least not to her. Ever.

She pulled open the curtains and looked out at the pool area. More luxury. Sometimes she felt like she was going to choke on the claustrophobic crush of wealth surrounding her in Cantara Hills.

She'd been serious when she'd told Caroline that she was thinking of moving. Of course her grandfather would have a cow. Stanton Kirkland had designed the Cantara Gardens condominiums. And for whatever reason, he liked the fact that his only granddaughter was living there.

A chiming noise interrupted her thoughts. It was the room phone. She walked over to the delicate rolltop desk and picked up the receiver.

"Victoria?"

"Yes?"

"Brody McQuade. I hope I didn't wake you."

You don't hope any such thing. If he were concerned about her getting enough sleep, he'd have waited another two hours to call.

"Did you…sleep okay?"

She smiled. There was nothing about this situation that was funny, but the idea that the unflappable lawman had no idea how to talk to her amused her. She just wished she knew what it was about her that bothered him so much.

"Not really. It was difficult to shut my brain off after everything that happened."

"Yeah. I need to talk to you this morning. Do you eat breakfast?"

"Every chance I get."

"Is it too early for you?"

She glanced at the clock on the bedside table. Eight-fifteen. "No. I'm up. Can you give me thirty minutes?"

"If you need more time—"

"I don't. Thanks."

"I'll knock on your door."

He hung up. Victoria looked at herself in the mirror and decided all she could do in half an hour was put her hair in a ponytail and grab some clothes. It wasn't like she was trying to impress him. It wasn't like she could.

By the time she'd dressed and brushed her hair, her nerves were thrumming in anticipation. She told herself she just wanted to get this over with. The sooner she was able to answer all Brody's questions, the sooner he could catch the killer and she could get back to her ordinary life.

She looked up from brushing her teeth and met her own gaze in the mirror. *Ordinary life. It* was all she'd ever wanted. An ordinary life. A boring life. And in the two years since her playboy fiancé had gone and stupidly gotten himself killed, she'd gotten her wish.

She rinsed her mouth and gathered her hair in a stretchy band. No way would she impress Brody this morning. Last night he'd given her exactly *no time* to pack. So she'd grabbed the first things she could get her hands on. Her makeup case, a handful of lingerie and a few items of clothing. She hadn't even had a chance to think about a scarf to cover up the bruises on her neck.

By the time she pulled on a pair of white Capri pants and a blue-and-white-striped top, a brisk knock sounded at her door. Her heart skipped as she fastened her watch around her wrist. Exactly thirty minutes. Why was she not surprised?

She walked through the sitting room and opened the double doors. There he was, dressed in crisp khaki pants and a fresh white shirt. He didn't have his hat on, and his hair was slightly damp.

He looked her up and down and one brow shot up. "Are you ready?"

"I only had a chance to grab a couple of things..." she started.

He shook his head and met her gaze, his eyes darker and more probing than usual. "You're fine. Fine." His gaze traced the line of her jaw and neck before meeting hers again.

"Don't you have a scarf or something?"

She touched her neck as the quiver inside her that had begun when he'd gathered her into his arms last night returned. She felt as graceless and awestruck as a teenager.

"No."

He reached into his pocket. "Here's a fresh handkerchief. Will that do?"

She took the snowy-white square of cloth and shook it out. "It's perfect." She rolled it up by opposite corners and tied it around her neck. He stepped backward to give her room to pass him. When he reached for the doors his shoulder brushed hers and a clean, fresh scent wafted across her nostrils.

A flash from last night hit her. He'd smelled like rain and body heat and wet clothes. This morning he still smelled like rain, and freshly pressed cotton and a hint of soap. Her knees went weak.

Just a reaction to the man who'd saved her life, she was sure. But as long as she had his handkerchief around her neck, she was doomed to be surrounded by his scent.

Brody escorted her to the dining room. It was bathed in sunlight from multiple sliding glass doors that led out to the Olympic-size pool. All the doors were open and a breeze stirred the sheer white curtains that ran on rods across the entire wall.

There were a few other diners, mostly business types who were either reading the newspaper as they ate or talking with colleagues.

As the hostess led them to their table, Victoria spotted Tammy Sutton and Margaret Hathaway with their heads together. Neither woman glanced up.

Tammy looked frustrated and nervous. Margaret's face was pale and her eyes were red.

Victoria touched Brody's arm. "I should speak to Tammy."

"No. Don't."

She frowned at him, but he'd pressed his hand against the small of her back and led her toward a table near the wall.

"We'll sit here," he told the hostess.

The young woman opened her mouth, but then thought better of whatever she'd been about to say. "Certainly, sir."

He seated Victoria with her back to Tammy and Margaret, then sat across from her.

"Why didn't—?"

"Shh." He held up a hand without looking at her.

He was eavesdropping on Tammy and Margaret.

Darn it. She was dying to turn around and see what he found so interesting about them. She could hear their voices, but they were nothing more than a murmur.

She watched his face, but she couldn't tell anything from his expression. He looked slightly bored, slightly impatient, like a man waiting for his first cup of coffee.

Victoria's fingers tingled and she felt prickles on the back of her neck. Just when she thought she couldn't sit still another second, Brody met her gaze, his eyes dark with warning. Then he pushed his chair back and stood.

"Victoria! My dear, how are you?"

Victoria looked up. "Tammy. I didn't see you come in."

"We've already eaten. You were engrossed with your breakfast companion and walked right by us." Tammy pressed her cheek against Victoria's and then held out her hand to Brody.

"Lieutenant McQuade. You're the Texas Ranger who's come to clean up our town, aren't you?"

"This small section of it, anyhow," he answered glibly.

Victoria turned her attention to Margaret Hathaway, who stood behind Tammy. "Margaret, how are you?"

Margaret smiled, but the sadness didn't leave her eyes. "I'm fine. I heard about your attack. I'm so glad you weren't hurt."

"Thanks. Me, too."

"You must call me, Victoria," Tammy said. "We didn't finish our conversation yesterday. I want to hear about everything." She looked at Victoria and inclined her head in Brody's direction.

"It's good to see you, Tammy, Margaret."

"Come on, Margaret. I'm going to be late for my spa appointment."

Brody nodded at them and then sat down.

The waitress, a young woman who had been hovering nearby waiting for the women to leave, poured coffee for them and took their orders.

Brody stirred a lot of sugar into his. He tasted it, then stirred in some more. He looked decidedly uncomfortable as he checked his watch and glanced around them.

"I'd be happy to talk to Sergeant Caldwell."

"No. You'll talk to me, whether you want to or not."

"It's not that. You obviously don't want to talk to me."

He took another swallow of coffee and looked at her over the rim of the cup. "You don't trust me."

Her pulse skipped. It was true. Although not in the way he probably meant. She didn't trust him because he disliked her so intensely. She couldn't blame him. She'd defended Gary Zelke, and it appeared that Brody would never get over that.

He set the coffee cup down and rested his hands on the table. He was one of the few people she'd ever seen who could sit with their hands still and relaxed. She hadn't taken a good look at his hands before. They were like the rest of him— large, spare, beautiful. Looking at them, she remembered their gentle touch on her neck.

She realized his comment about her not trusting him still hovered, unanswered, in the air.

She shrugged. "I know how you feel about me."

"I told you before, my personal feelings don't enter into this. You're my only witness—my only link to this guy. And I'm not about to let him get to you."

"Thank you for that," she said wryly, just as the waitress brought their food.

Brody dug right into his eggs and hash browns.

Victoria broke apart her cranberry muffin and buttered it, but she wasn't hungry. "Well?" she said.

Brody looked up, one brow raised. "Well what?"

"What were Tammy and Margaret saying?"

"What makes you think I know?"

"Don't give me that." She waved the buttered piece of muffin. "You were listening—eavesdropping. It was killing me that I couldn't turn around. What did you hear?"

"How are they connected?"

"How come you answer every single question with a question?"

"Do I do that?"

There was that twinkle again. She bit her lip to keep from laughing. "You know you do."

"So…Tammy and Margaret?" he asked.

"Well, I guess they're about the same age, so maybe they went to school together. Margaret is Link Hathaway's daughter, and Link is on the city planning board with Kenneth."

"Yeah. They're both members of the Cantara Hills Home-owners' Association, too. I'm meeting with them this after-noon about buying a new security system for the condos."

He took a swig of coffee. "Whose baby would Tammy and Margaret be talking about?"

"Baby?" Victoria dusted muffin crumbs off her fingers. "I have no idea. Neither Tammy nor Margaret have ever had a child. Margaret's never been married." She leaned forward. "What did they say?"

"I didn't catch much of it. Tammy was doing most of the talking and Margaret was upset."

"Who said something about a baby?"

"Tammy. She said, 'Get the baby,' or 'It's the baby.' I couldn't tell exactly. But she was ticked off, and Margaret looked miserable."

"There's a couple who live near Taylor Landis, I think, who're pregnant. Maybe Tammy and Margaret are planning a baby shower. You want me to see what I can find out?"

"No." Brody scowled. "You're not going to do anything except stay put. I need you alive and well. You're my only witness."

"I won't be well if you keep me locked in that room. I'll be out of my mind."

"You'll manage. Now I've got a few more questions for

you. What do you know about the bottle of oil that was smashed at the bottom of your stairs?"

"I threw it. I was hoping it would slow him down."

Brody nodded. "It not only slowed him down, it gave us some good footprints."

Victoria felt a small triumph. "I'm glad. I felt so helpless, so much like a victim. I'm glad something I did helped."

He picked up his mug and drank. "You did good. We can get an idea of his size and weight from the print."

The wave of pride and pleasure that swept through her at his words warmed her cheeks. She took a drink of ice water, hoping he hadn't noticed her blush.

He was filling his fork with hash browns. "What do you know about Amanda Winger?" he asked.

"She's Tammy Sutton's mother."

"I got that much. Do you know her?"

Victoria speared a pineapple wedge from her plate of fresh fruit. "Not really. We speak. I don't think she's comfortable in her condo. She had money stolen, didn't she?"

He nodded and didn't say anything else until he'd finished eating. Then he picked up the coffeepot from the nearby stand and poured himself and her another cup of coffee. He loaded his up with sugar again.

"You always use that much sugar?"

"Yeah, why?"

"I'm surprised you're not climbing the walls."

He shrugged. "Do you know anything about her comings and goings?"

"Who? Mrs. Winger? Not really. Why?"

"On the night you were attacked she used her access card twice. Three times on the night Briggs was killed and once when Zelke was killed."

"I don't understand. She's a victim, too. Had five thousand dollars stolen."

"Right. So she says. She can't prove she had the money, and she can't prove anyone was in her apartment. There was no physical evidence found in any of the apartments of victims who were gone at the time of the break-ins."

"Are you suggesting *she* killed Gary or Trent? That's ridiculous. I can guarantee you a small woman in her seventies did not attack me."

His eyes snapped. "I'm not suggesting she did. I think she loaned somebody her card."

"Tammy?"

"Didn't you tell me it was a man who attacked you? It would help a lot if I could eliminate the females, but since anyone could have given the killer their card, I can't rule out even a small, seventy-eight-year-old woman. Trouble is, when I tried to talk to her, she told me her daughter made her promise not to answer any questions."

"I've visited her a couple of times," Victoria said. "I took her some flowers once when she was sick. She'll talk to me."

"I told you, you're not talking to anyone. No." Brody tossed down his napkin. "You want more coffee?"

Victoria shook her head. He topped off his cup again, then reached for the sugar bowl. He checked his hand in midair, glanced at her and left the bowl sitting there. He drank his coffee black.

She hid a smile. "Come on, Brody, it makes sense. I could go talk to her, she'll ask me if I'm okay and I can mention how the man got in. I'll bet you I can get her to tell me about her comings and goings."

He shook his head, but before he could speak, she went

on, "You have to let me help. I can't just sit in that sterile suite and do nothing."

"You don't have any briefs you can work on?"

"In my job I spend most of my time meeting with clients and advising them on their businesses or investments. I do most of my work face-to-face."

"Then I guess you'd better get used to doing nothing."

Victoria leaned forward and put her hand on Brody's where it rested next to his cup. "Please let me help. I can talk to her."

Brody pinned her with his dark gaze. Then he looked down at her hand on his.

Her face heated again. She pulled her hand back.

"I still have about twenty or so people to talk to at the condos," he said. "You come with me. You see Mrs. Winger, and then you call my cell phone and I'll bring you back here. You don't go anywhere else. You don't talk to anyone else. Got it?"

Victoria breathed a sigh of relief. Talking to Mrs. Winger wasn't the most exciting way to spend a morning, but at least she wouldn't be stuck in the country club where her choices were to watch daytime television or sit out in the sun. "Yes, sir."

"Well, well."

Brody winced and quelled an urge to groan. He'd know that whiny voice anywhere. He tore his gaze away from Victoria's sparkling gaze to meet the beady brown eyes of Carlson Woodward, tennis pro.

What a joke. Whiny, spoiled Carlson being a pro at *any*thing was worthy of a belly laugh. Brody cut his eyes over to Carlson's too-tanned legs sticking out from under a pair of white shorts. He could see the streaks of self-tanning stuff that had rubbed off on the hem of the shorts.

He'd known Carlson was working at the country club, but until now he hadn't run into him. He'd been thankful for that. He wasn't pleased that Carlson had found him with Victoria.

"If it's not the big bad Texas Ranger, Mr. Brody McQuade." Carlson's too-full, too-pouty lips curved into a sinister smile. "My dear foster brother. I heard you were investigating the rampant terror engulfing Cantara Gardens. And now here you are, caught in an early-morning assignation with the lovely Victoria Kirkland."

Carlson stepped over and held out his hand to Victoria. After a swift glance at Brody, she reluctantly offered her hand. Carlson grasped it and bowed over it. Brody nearly laughed at the moue of distaste that marred her features as his lips touched her skin.

For himself, Brody wanted nothing more than to knock the smirking Lothario across the room. He had to unclench his fist.

He had no idea how Carlson got women to fall for him and he didn't want to know. But he was glad Victoria had better sense than to be charmed by him.

Victoria took her hand back as quickly as she could. Carlson turned his smug smile toward Brody, missing Victoria's swipe of her napkin across the back of her hand.

"I heard about the near tragedy. Lucky you were there to save our damsel in distress." He picked an invisible speck of lint off his white polo shirt. "I know everyone in the condos of course, so if you need anything—anything at all, Brody—please just call on me."

He adjusted a terry cloth wristband and hiked the strap of his tennis-racket bag higher on his shoulder. "Meanwhile, toodles."

Brody wrapped his hand around his cup, ignoring the

handle, and drank a big swallow, hoping it would wash away the bad taste Carlson left in his mouth.

"Foster brother?" Victoria was still scrubbing at her hand. "What's that about?"

Brody clenched his jaw. He was just about to tell her it was none of her business, not because it wasn't, but because he was thoroughly PO'd from just seeing Carlson. He needed her cooperation, however. It would complicate his life a *lot* to have her angry with him.

Not his life—his *job,* he corrected himself.

"Carlson's the natural son of my foster parents." He heard the bite in his voice.

"Foster parents? Oh, I'm so sorry. Your parents died?"

"It's a long, sad story. Come on. I'll take you to your penthouse to get some more clothes, then we can arrange for you to talk to Mrs. Winger." Brody stood and held her chair.

At the door to her suite, she thought of something and turned, catching Brody too close for comfort. "I just remembered, I see Carlson at the condos all the time."

"His name isn't on my list of tenants."

She shook her head with a little smile. "No. A tennis pro's salary, even here, wouldn't be enough to rent an apartment in Cantara Gardens."

Despite his long-standing animosity toward Carlson, Brody bristled at the implication of the class differences between those who lived in Cantara Hills and those who just worked there.

"So what's his business at the condos?" he asked, a hard edge he hadn't intended darkening his tone.

Her eyes widened and she moistened her lips. "It's just that I thought you might find this important. I wasn't trying to insult your foster brother."

"Trust me, insulting Carlson is one of my favorite pastimes. What about him in the condos?"

Victoria glanced up and down the hall. Then she leaned in and lifted her chin so she was speaking close to his ear. "I think he gives *private* lessons to some of the women. I've seen him use an access card to get through the gate."

Brody lifted his head. "Private lessons? To whom?"

"Well, Jane Majorsky, for one. She's the only one I've actually seen with him. I could talk to her, too, while I'm there talking with Mrs. Winger."

"Don't even think about it. You won't have time. So you said you've seen him teaching tennis lessons to *some* of the women."

"That's not what I said."

Brody clenched his jaw. *Lawyers.* "All right, Madame Attorney. What exactly did you say?"

"I said I think he's giving *private lessons.* I meant it as a euphemism. You know, a—"

"I know. So you're saying Carlson has access to the condos. You're saying he could be the killer."

IT WAS ALMOST DARK by the time Brody left the Cantara Hills home of Kenneth Sutton, where he'd met with the homeowners' association. And he was steaming.

He'd presented a bulletproof case for upgrading Cantara Gardens' security system, including a better tracking system for access cards, recording of duplicate cards, an alert for more than one entry in a three-hour period, plus a number of other measures to ensure the safety of the tenants.

But to a man, the board had balked at more expensive and intrusive precautions. Kenneth Sutton had been the loudest.

Cantara Hills was a peaceful community made up of responsible pillars of business and society in San Antonio, Sutton had argued. He didn't want the people who lived there to be treated like prisoners.

Brody had hammered back with the obvious—eight break-ins resulting in two murders, as well as two attempts on Victoria Kirkland's life, all taking place in Cantara Gardens Condos. And all within the past eight months.

It had taken three hours to wrangle an agreement to replace all security cards and institute a no-duplicate-card policy in Cantara Gardens.

That wasn't his only frustration of the day, either. He'd gotten Victoria back to the Country Club after she'd talked with Mrs. Winger, and had told Egan to keep an eye on her.

Once he'd realized how long the meeting with the home-owners' association was going to take, he'd called Egan to let him know, but the sergeant had bad news for him. He'd been called back to Austin to be deposed in a pending case and was already on his way.

Victoria had been there at the country club for two hours alone. Brody was antsy to get back and make sure she was okay.

As he walked across the massive paved driveway, a breeze kicked up and he smelled rain in the air. He surveyed the dozen or so luxury vehicles in Sutton's driveway. They ranged from a vintage Town Car to a sparkling new Mercedes Cabriolet convertible.

Six drivers were there, waiting for their bosses. They leaned against the cars shooting the breeze, or inspecting the polished surface with a snowy white rag in hand, or just staring into space.

Brody knew the first driver. It was Walt Caldwell, Egan's father. He'd worked as a chauffeur for Link Hathaway for as long as Brody could remember. And Egan had always resented him.

Walt looked up as Brody approached. Then he looked down at his feet and folded his arms. He wasn't sure whether he was supposed to acknowledge that he knew Brody.

"Mr. Caldwell," Brody said, stepping up to him and holding out his hand. "How've you been?"

Walt straightened and shook Brody's hand, still without looking him straight in the eye. "Not too bad. I hear you're investigating those killings over at the condos."

"That's right. Egan's here, too."

"That boy. I haven't seen him in…well, in a long time. He doing okay?"

"Yeah," Brody answered. "He's doing good." He chatted with Walt for a few minutes about the break-ins. Walt knew most of the people involved.

"The night of the party, you drove Hathaway to Taylor Landis's house?"

Walt nodded and looked down at his feet again. "Listen, Brody—Lieutenant—I'm really sorry about your sister."

Brody winced internally. "Thanks. I appreciate that. See anything unusual that night?"

"Not really." Walt kept his eyes on his shoes. "All I know is a bunch of people left really fast, around eleven."

"Like who?"

"The blond lawyer and her lawyer friend in her new Lexus. Ms. Stallings in that Corvette with…you know, with Kimberly, and a couple more people."

"When did Hathaway leave?"

"Not till later. Around 1:00 a.m. or so."

"Who else was here? Any of these guys?" Brody nodded toward the other vehicles.

Walt shifted and crossed his arms. "Can't say."

"Can't or won't?"

"Don't remember."

"Come on, Mr. Caldwell. You know I can have the police bring you in and question you. Maybe that'll jog your memory."

Walt shrugged. "Whatever you got to do."

"We'll see. If your memory comes back, give me a call." Brody flipped Walt a business card, turned on his heel and walked down the row of cars.

He recognized the city-owned license plate of the mayor's car, and the vanity plates on Devon Goldenrod's vintage Town Car. But he wasn't interested in either of them. At least not yet.

As the driver of a new Mercedes Cabriolet raised its convertible top in preparation for the coming rain, Brody headed toward the four-car garage on the west side of the house. A man dressed in dark-blue livery was putting the last polish on a black Jaguar. Brody strolled over.

"Looks good." He crossed his arms and leaned against the driver's side door. It wasn't much of a stretch to figure that the Jag was Kenneth Sutton's. The chauffeur looked very much at home compared to the other drivers.

"Thanks," the man muttered, rubbing at an invisible smudge on the hood. "Mind not leaning?"

Brody didn't move. He assessed the driver. At first glance he seemed fairly typical of the usual driver for a wealthy businessman. He was relatively young, maybe late thirties, and Hispanic, with the high cheekbones that hinted at some Native American in his ancestry.

Most of the other drivers were dressed in business suits or jackets and slacks, but this man, like Walt Caldwell, wore full livery. And unlike the others' bored expressions, this man's sharp black eyes missed nothing.

He reached to flick away a speck of dust from the hood, and Brody saw a telltale bulge at the small of his back. He was carrying.

Not just a driver. A bodyguard.

Just as the chauffeur took a step toward him, a warning look in his eye, Brody casually straightened and stepped away from the car. He didn't want to antagonize the man. He wanted information.

"I'm Brody McQuade. I'm looking into the break-ins at Cantara Gardens."

The man nodded and buffed the door where Brody had leaned. "Texas Ranger." His tone was noncommittal.

"And you are…?"

No answer. More buffing.

Brody adjusted his stance and rested his palm on the handle of his holstered gun.

"Montoya. Vincent." Montoya tossed the buffing rag onto the hood of the car, where it slid across the immaculate surface, and crossed his arms. He stood balanced on both feet and looking out across Sutton's manicured lawn.

Brody recrossed his arms and looked in the same direction. "How long have you been driving for Mr. Sutton?"

"A year."

"So you drove him to the Christmas party at Taylor Landis's estate?"

No answer.

"And you waited there for him?"

"That's what he pays me for."

"You're not just a driver, are you?"

"You have a good eye."

"It pays, in my business."

"Yes. I understand. It pays in mine, too."

Brody pushed the brim of his hat up slightly. "Mr. Sutton have a lot of enemies?"

"I drive, and when I drive, I am responsible for Mr. Sutton's safety."

Brody smiled inwardly. Montoya was a cagey one. "Do you drive Mrs. Sutton, too?"

"Mrs. Sutton enjoys her Jaguar."

"So you have a lot of downtime."

Montoya retrieved his buffing rag and went back to polishing the immaculate surface of the Jaguar. "I'm involved in many things."

I'll bet. "Any of them take you to Cantara Gardens Condos?"

Montoya shrugged and tugged his cap down over his eyes. "Mr. Sutton has a lot of business interests in this area. Now I need to check the oil, and gas up the car. Mr. and Mrs. Sutton are going out to dinner."

Brody pulled the brim of his hat down. He removed a card from his breast pocket. "If you think of anything you've noticed that could present a danger to your boss or any of the residents, give me a call."

"No problem."

Brody walked on down the driveway, got into his Jeep and glanced in the rearview mirror. He'd given Montoya a perfect opportunity to mention Tammy Sutton's mother, but he hadn't. Maybe Montoya did have some business, legitimate or otherwise, at the condos.

He started the engine and pulled out. Most of the drivers were unconcerned with him. Only two, Walt Caldwell and Vincent Montoya, watched him leave. Did they have reason to keep up with his movements? Brody filed that information away as he pulled out onto the highway and dug into his pocket for his cell phone.

He called Victoria. "Where are you?"

"In the suite. I just got out of the shower and am about to watch a rerun of *Friends*."

She sounded totally disgusted and bored. It almost made him smile. "Good. I assume you had a good talk with Amanda Winger?"

"Yes. And Byron Dalloway. Jane Majorsky wasn't home."

"You weren't supposed to talk to anyone else."

"I had plenty of time while I was waiting for you."

"Yeah, sorry. I got held up. I've got some more questions for you, and I want to hear about Winger—" he took an irritated breath "—and Dalloway. Have you eaten?"

"Not since breakfast."

"I've got to shower, then I'll come get you. Is pizza okay?"

"Sausage and mushroom?"

"Pepperoni and extra cheese." For some reason he got a kick out of baiting her. He couldn't care less what kind of pizza he ate. Pizza was pizza. His favorite part about it was that it appeared at the door and the packaging was disposable.

He heard her sigh. "Okay. Pepperoni and extra cheese."

"Good. Stay in your suite with the doors locked until I get there."

"We're going out?" she asked hopefully.

"Just down the hall to my suite. Come as you are."

There was a pause on the other end of his phone. Then, "Probably not a good idea."

His mouth went dry. He'd seen her in a slinky nightgown and slinky satin pajamas. What could she possibly have on that was more revealing?

Just got out of the shower, she'd said. Now his brain answered *Nothing* as it zeroed in on the memory of the faint shadow between her breasts and the subtle outline of nipples beneath the pale ivory gown she'd had on.

Whoa! He reined in his escalating libido. "Uh, okay. Something comfortable, then. I'm ordering in."

He heard a muffled noise. Was she laughing at him?

"I'll see you in forty-five minutes," he snapped, and shut off his phone.

VICTORIA PACED HER bedroom floor. It had been forty-six minutes since Brody had hung up. He was late. She'd had him figured for a guy who was never late.

The phone had rung just as she was getting out of the shower. When he'd said *Come as you are,* she'd been dripping wet with a towel wrapped around her. The thought of him seeing her like that sent ripples of desire down to the deepest part of her.

She glanced at the table where a foil-covered tray sat. Feeling silly and a little embarrassed, she picked it up and sat it on the floor on the far side of the bed, near the French doors. Brody didn't need to know she'd ordered a cold lobster salad from the kitchen that had come just before she'd jumped into the shower. She told herself pizza sounded much better.

Just as she debated covering the tray with the curtains, a knock sounded.

Relief tingled through her, irritating her. She didn't like how much she'd come to depend on Brody being there for her. Shaking her head and pressing her lips together, she opened the door—and stifled a gasp.

"Hello, Victoria." Carlson Woodward took a step forward. He smiled, parting his too-full lips and baring his too-white teeth.

Victoria tried to push the door closed, but Carlson didn't move. The look he gave her sent nauseating chills down her spine and made her shudder. Apprehension sped up her heartbeat. She looked beyond him.

Where was Brody?

Carlson leered at her. "I assume you were expecting someone else?"

Chapter Six

"What do you want?" Victoria gripped the door handle, but Carlson's weight kept her from pushing it closed. He gave the door a little shove and stepped into her room. She had to back up or find herself mere inches away from his dissipated face.

"Now, Victoria, be nice. Here I am taking the time to check on you. I've been worried about you, and you treat me like this."

She gritted her teeth. She'd never spoken more than a few words to Carlson, mainly *hi* and *how are you*. But she could see why Brody didn't like his foster brother. He was creepy, and he practically oozed slime.

"I'm expecting company." She looked at her watch. "Any second now."

Carlson had changed from his tennis whites to a pair of white dress slacks, a red polo shirt and a blue-and-white-striped sweater that he'd flung over his shoulders and tied in front by the sleeves. The outfit was impeccable and obviously expensive, but on him it looked like a costume.

Still, it didn't decrease the air of menace that emanated from him.

"Now that definitely is disappointing. I was going to ask

you to have dinner with me. We've never had the chance to get to know each other, and that's a shame." His intense gaze never left hers. And he never blinked. "I'd love to hear about your attack."

He took another step forward. Victoria backed up a step. Her apprehension was climbing like a cartoon thermometer about to explode out the top. When the top blew off, she wasn't sure what she would do. All she knew was that she was trapped in her room by a very scary man.

Carlson leaned toward her and she got a whiff of his cologne. *Torture.* Terror streaked through her. The same scent as the killer. "You…" she started, but her throat seized. She swallowed. "You need to leave."

Carlson's smile widened and he reached behind him to push the door closed, but just as he touched it, it flew wide open and slammed against the wall.

Brody.

Thank God. Victoria almost cried with relief. Her shaky legs barely held her up as the tension drained away and her head stopped pounding. She'd been so scared.

"What the hell's going on here?"

The color drained from Carlson's face, making him look like a kabuki dancer with those pink lips and black eyes.

"B-Brody," he stammered. "I thought Victoria might want to get out for a while. I was offering to take her to dinner."

Brody's eyes met hers and a jaw muscle twitched. "She's having dinner with me."

Carlson pasted on a smile and held out his hand toward Victoria. This time she didn't offer hers.

A dangerous glint sparked in his eyes as he turned the gesture into a little affected bow. "Another time, then. Now if you'll excuse me…"

Brody stood his ground, forcing Carlson to go around him. Just before Carlson rounded the corner, he shot Brody a look that sent fear skittering down Victoria's spine. If looks could kill, Brody McQuade would be dead.

"Dear heavens," she whispered, putting her hand over her mouth.

Brody crossed to her side. "Are you okay? He didn't do anything, did he?"

She shook her head. "He's so...the look he just gave you..." She was bordering on a meltdown. She swallowed and tried again. "He looked like he wanted to kill you."

Brody just shrugged. "He always has."

She couldn't suppress a shudder. "He has the creepiest eyes I've ever seen."

Brody squeezed her shoulder reassuringly. The warmth of his hand banished the chill that had collected inside her in the presence of Carlson Woodward. "Come on. Let's go eat some pizza."

Victoria blew out a long breath and took her first good look at Brody. He had on jeans. And a white T-shirt that hinted at the planed abs she'd felt when she'd vaulted into his arms the night before. His hair was damp and bore the furrows of his comb.

He'd just showered, too. Her pulse jumped and her heart leaped. She swallowed.

When he lifted his head, she was struck, just like every other time, by the intensity in his dark eyes. For a couple of seconds he took in her appearance. The feel of his gaze on her breasts and waist and below sent a thrill sliding along her nerve endings. She suppressed a shiver.

What was he looking at? Of all the clothes she'd brought with her from her penthouse, she'd chosen the least sexy. A pair of baggy madras shorts and an oversize T-shirt that read Take a Walk on the Riverwalk. She'd twisted her hair up and caught it with a clip, and she hadn't put on any makeup.

"Ready?"

"Yes. I wore loose shorts so I can eat a lot of pizza." She smiled, but his attention was on closing her door and checking to make sure it was locked.

"Pizza's not here yet. It should be coming in a few minutes." He put his hand on the small of her back as they walked the few doors down to his suite.

She took a deep breath, trying to stop the tingling inside her. His fresh-rain scent mingled with the rose-scented body wash she'd used. The mixture was heady and titillating. An image of them in the shower with water streaming down their faces and suds sliding over their slick skin assaulted her inner vision.

"What?" he said.

Oh no. Had she said something? Made a noise? "What?" she countered.

He shrugged. "I don't know. I thought you said something."

"No. No. I was just..." She had no idea how to finish the sentence.

Then she remembered Carlson's cologne. "Oh, Brody." She grabbed his arm.

"It's okay. You're fine."

"No. I mean, I know. It's Carlson. He had on the same cologne as the attacker—the same as my ex-fiancé."

Brody stopped in the middle of the hall and looked both ways. "Are you sure?"

She nodded, but immediately questioned herself. "It was pretty strong. But there was something a little off about the smell."

"Off? You mean it smelled different on Carlson? That doesn't surprise me, since he's a skunk."

"It had more to do with the undertone. It seemed a little stale or old or something. Not like…my attacker and not like my ex."

"Humph. Probably fake, knowing Carlson."

"An impostor fragrance," she said. "That's probably it. I'll have to get some of both and compare them."

"Here we go." He unlocked the door and stood back. She stepped into a large conference room with three doors spaced equally on the far wall.

A huge mahogany table filled most of one side of the room, and a wet bar and refrigerator plus a sofa and chairs occupied the other side.

Behind the mahogany table stood a whiteboard with bold black writing all over it. She saw several names she recognized, including her own. "What's this?" she asked.

Brody closed the door and gestured for her to sit at the table. "What do you want to drink?"

Irritation pricked at her chest. He wasn't going to answer her. She wanted to jump up and yell at him, but she didn't. "What have you got?"

He opened the refrigerator. "The club keeps us stocked. Just about anything you want, from water to beer to juices." He reached in and pulled out a beer and held it up.

"I never really developed a taste for beer," she said. "Is there any wine?"

He sent her a look that telegraphed what he thought about a woman who didn't like beer, then pulled out a six-pack of single-serving wine bottles. "White zinfandel?"

"Perfect." She didn't like the way he made her feel like a prima donna. "You know, not liking beer is just a personal thing. It has nothing to do with money."

He popped the top on his beer and took a long swallow. "I didn't say it did."

No, but his tone did.

He brought a bottle of the wine and a glass to the table. "There you go. White zinfandel for the lady."

Victoria seethed, knowing he was baiting her. But before she could say anything, he spoke.

"So could Carlson be your attacker?"

She wrapped her arms protectively around her middle. "I don't think so. He's…he doesn't look like he weighs enough. The man was—" she shrugged "—bulkier. Plus, that cologne wasn't right."

"I'm going to have him pulled in, anyway. He could use being brought down a peg or two."

"How did your meeting go with the homeowners' association? I should have warned you, they probably don't like beer, either. You know how we trust-fund babies can be."

Brody turned back to the refrigerator. Hearing her use the term he'd thought of the first time he'd seen her made his cheeks burn. Was it that obvious how he felt about the idle rich?

Goodness knew his parents fit that category. Even at eleven he'd understood how selfish they'd been, flying off to obscure and dangerous places, leaving their two small children with nannies. When their private plane crashed into the side of a mountain in Nepal, he'd decided then and there that money did nothing but break hearts.

But by the time he was twenty-five and able to draw from the trust, Kimmie was getting ready for college, so he'd altered his oath never to touch their inheritance, and used some of the money to give her the best education it could buy.

"People who have always been rich don't understand the

world the way ordinary people do. They don't know what it's like to know they've earned their place rather than having it handed to them. They think they can do anything and not be touched. They think they're immortal."

He grabbed a second beer and brought it to the table.

Victoria was studying him with her head slightly cocked to one side. "Who are you talking about?"

He took another long swallow of beer as he replayed what he'd just said. *Crap*. He hadn't meant to go on like that. "Nobody. Just something I heard someone say once."

Victoria frowned and opened her mouth, but a pounding on the door saved him from whatever she'd been about to say.

"Pizza," he said unnecessarily. When he got to the door, he put his right hand behind his back.

Victoria noticed the bulge of a gun under his T-shirt.

"Yeah?" he called out.

"Pizza delivery."

He opened the door, dug cash out of his pocket, handed it to the pimply kid and took the box from him.

He kicked the door closed and set the box on the table in front of Victoria. Then he took the paddle holster and gun and laid them on a side table.

She opened the top. "Mushroom and sausage!"

His eyes twinkled at her surprise. "I'm not a complete ogre."

She grabbed a slice and took a big bite.

"No, I can see that you're not complete," she mumbled as she chewed. "You still need some work." She could swear she saw him clamp his jaw to keep from smiling. As she took a second bite, she made herself a promise. Before this was all over, she *would* make Brody McQuade laugh.

Victoria was fascinated by the way he ate. She'd noticed

it in men before. He concentrated on eating until he was finished. Assessing his body, she wondered where he put it. His lean physique didn't appear to have any room for four slices of pizza. Her grandmother would have said he had a hollow leg.

He put down the last piece of crust and finished his beer. "So what did Amanda Winger say?"

Typical. No small talk, certainly nothing personal. "At first she didn't want to let me in. She didn't recognize me. But I told her my apartment was broken into, also, and that I knew Tammy."

Brody picked up the pizza box and tossed it into the trash. "You want to sit on the couch?"

Victoria frowned at him. What was he trying to do? This was a business meeting. In her world, and she suspected in his, business was carried on at polished wood conference tables. "Why?"

He gave her a puzzled look. "Because it's more comfortable."

"Oh, of course. Sure." She picked up her wineglass and walked across the room to the sofa. She settled in and sipped at her wine.

Brody sat on the other end. "What did she say about her access card?"

"It took a while to get her around to talking about that. I spent quite some time telling her about my attack and listening to her complain about Tammy wanting to buy her a better security system. Finally that led to talking about how the attacker got in."

Brody shifted impatiently. "Yeah? And *then* did you ask about her card?"

"It was what we expected. She finally admitted she'd given Tammy a card and told the manager she'd misplaced hers."

"That explains all those comings and goings. What about Kenneth Sutton?"

"I asked her, but she said no. Just Tammy. I guess Kenneth could use Tammy's card."

"I guess. Or she was lying."

"Why would she lie about that? Or about anything. She seems so sweet."

Brody sent her a sidelong glance. "Everybody lies."

"Wow. That's pretty cynical."

He shook his head. Was she really that trusting? He was going to have to watch her closely. "It's not cynical. It's the way the world is."

"Still, what about a master access card? Maybe the manager gave Kenneth a master."

"Nope. The masters show up as 'master' on the computer."

"And there's not enough use of the master to account for the times of the break-ins?"

Brody shoved himself up off the couch. "Not nearly enough. Take a look." He walked over to the whiteboard where he and Hayes had tracked the movements of the residents.

"What *is* all this?" she asked, stepping up beside him.

"A grid showing all the Cantara Gardens residents who used their access cards on the nights of the attacks."

"You just have the three nights on here. What about the other break-ins, where nobody was home?"

Brody assessed her. He liked her logical mind. She was a lot like him, fitting the pieces together carefully and methodically. He'd bet she was a whiz with a jigsaw puzzle. "I've got them on paper. The pattern is the same."

She studied the board for a few seconds. "I see what you mean about Mrs. Winger's comings and goings."

"Did you ask her about the cologne?"

She nodded. "She didn't remember anything, but she said she uses an inhaler, and it's damaged her sense of smell."

"What about Dalloway? Since you managed to find the time to talk to him, too."

"Have you never met him?"

Brody shook his head. "He wasn't in. I tried four or five times in the past couple of days, but he's always out."

"Well, he was in today. You should see his apartment. You literally could eat off the floors, and the entire place is spotless—dustless. He's got scented candles and air fresheners everywhere."

"So he didn't notice the cologne, either. What else did he say?"

"According to Byron, the humidor is extremely valuable. He claims it's from the seventeenth century. He showed me where he kept it on his mantel. He nearly cried."

"The police report stated that he valued the thing at several thousand dollars, but he couldn't provide proof he had it."

"Apparently his mother had it appraised years ago, and the total was something in the neighborhood of ten thousand dollars. But the certified appraisal was destroyed when his mother's house burned. He told me he polished it every day."

Brody looked at her. "Every day?"

"Yes. With lemon oil." She took a deep breath. "Brody, I think you should let me go back and talk to Jane Majorsky."

Brody sent her a glare. "Not a chance. So whoever stole the humidor probably has his fingerprints all over it." In spite of his determination to stay focused and not get his hopes up, Brody's heart leaped. "If Hayes can find that humidor, we could have our killer."

Chapter Seven

Victoria shivered at the notion of the brute who'd tried to strangle her holding the polished humidor in his murderous hands. "How can Hayes find it?"

"I'm betting that the guy's only motive for stealing the items was to create a red herring to throw us off. If he's a burglar who killed in desperation because he got caught, that's one thing."

"But you think the burglaries were committed to cover up the murders." She shivered again. "I still don't understand how that's going to help Hayes find the humidor."

"This guy doesn't have any use for those items. But everybody wants more money."

There was that tone again. What was it with Brody and money?

"I'm counting on them showing up in a pawnshop or an antiques store sooner or later—hopefully sooner," he continued. "I've got Hayes out scouring the city. If that humidor is out there, he'll find it."

His dark eyes gave her the once-over, stopping at her face. "Come on, I'll take you back to your room. You look like you could use some sleep."

"Thanks," she said wryly.

Brody scowled. "All I meant was you look tired—"

"Please." She held up her hands. "Stop now. You're killing me with compliments. Thanks for the pizza. I think I can make it ten steps up the hall to my door."

"No. I'll walk you back there and wait until you lock the dead bolt."

"Fine, then. Are you sure you can stand having me two whole rooms away? Why don't you just lock me in your bedroom so you'll have me right where you want me?"

His gaze snapped to hers and she realized what she'd said. It shouldn't have been a big deal. It should have been just a friendly joke, poking fun at his insistence on keeping such a close eye on her.

But that *thing* between them rose up like a dragon, assaulting them with the burning fire of lust. Victoria's face felt as if the dragon's breath had touched it. She knew her cheeks were red with embarrassment.

Brody, on the other hand, was staring at her as if she'd just stripped naked in front of him. In a metaphorical sense she had. Her reaction to her own words was all too revealing. She knew it. And worse, he knew she knew it.

She had no idea how long they stood there silently with her words between them.

She watched emotions chase each other across his face— surprise, lust, embarrassment, even curiosity. Dear heavens, was he wondering what it would be like to make love with her? Because that was exactly what she couldn't get out of her mind.

He cleared his throat and took a step backward—his way of distancing himself. She knew it well already.

"Let's go," he said.

"Right. Let's."

Brody opened the door and held it for her. When she passed him she breathed in his rain-fresh scent. Oh man, she was going to have to stop doing that. She wished she could ask him to stop bathing, or at least stop using that soap or shampoo—whatever it was—because it acted on her like an aphrodisiac.

Once she stepped out into the hall, she was glad he was walking with her. The guest wing of the country club had only faint night-lights over each door. Shadows lurked in alcoves and the side halls that led out to the pool area.

She'd never been afraid of the dark, but the attack on her had changed all that. She felt Brody's hand on the small of her back and her knees went weak.

Gratitude, she told herself. She was grateful that his intense, conscientious nature made him obsessive about her safety.

At her door she pulled her card out of her shorts pocket. He reached around and took it from her hand. For a brief instant his heat surrounded her. Not just his hand on hers but his bare arm against her shoulder, his body so close she could feel his life force through the two layers of cotton that was all that separated them.

A sweet ache traveled from her hand up her arm and all the way through her. She let him take her card. Then she did something she never thought she would do. If anyone had suggested it two days ago when she'd first met him, she'd have scoffed.

She turned toward him. When her breasts brushed his chest, she didn't pull away. Even more amazing, neither did he. Then she stood on tiptoe and pressed her cheek against his—torturing herself with his scent.

"Thank you," she whispered.

He stiffened, and she knew in the next instant he'd be at least two feet from her. But to her surprise he didn't move. Instead, he looked down at her, his eyes the color of rich, dark chocolate.

"Vic," he whispered. "Don't get the wrong idea."

Her cheeks heated again. What an idiot she was. She moved to step back, but his arm circled her, stopping her.

"I'm sorry, Brody. I didn't mean—"

He stopped her from talking by kissing her—sort of. He lowered his head enough that she could imagine she felt his lips on hers. His warm breath slid across her mouth like a butterfly's wing. She shivered and closed her eyes. At that moment she couldn't make herself care that she was throwing herself at him. She'd never in her life felt as safe, as protected, as turned on, as she did right then.

Then his lips did touch hers and she knew what had gone before *was* imagination because this—this was the real thing.

His mouth was firm, demanding, yet in its own way gentle. He didn't force the kiss, but he didn't hesitate, either. It was perfect—a perfect instant that held her in an erotic world between earth and heaven.

She had no concept of time passing, although she was aware of his arm tightening, pulling her closer. When he ended the kiss, it was all she could do to keep from moaning in frustration.

He pressed his forehead against hers. "I can't do this. I need all my senses, all my energy, to track down the killer. I don't want you to think…"

"Don't worry," she said quickly. "I don't think anything. I'm a big girl."

"Look, Vic, it's not—"

A noise cut off his words, like metal against metal. Brody froze, listening.

Victoria moved but he stayed her with a hand.

Crap! He didn't have his gun. "Stand back," he whispered. "If anything happens, run for the office and call 9-1-1."

"What are you—"

He silenced her with a gesture. Then he rammed the card into the slot and shoved the door open, his pulse pounding.

Nothing. There was nobody in the room. But the French doors were open and the gauzy curtains ruffled slightly in the breeze.

"Son of a—" he muttered. Someone had broken into her room.

He stepped over the spilled room-service tray and through the doors, then looked around, but as he expected, the pool area was deserted. Whoever had broken in was gone.

"Brody?"

He turned. Victoria was standing in the doorway.

"I told you to stay back. Did you leave the French doors unlocked?" He knew the answer. She wasn't the kind of person to forget to lock up.

"Of course not," she said.

He pulled his cell phone out of his pocket and hit a number. "Sergeant Deason, McQuade. Just had a break-in here at the Country Club. Get your closest units over here. Stop all vehicles leaving the area. And send some officers to question the guests and the staff."

Victoria's eyes were wide and shocked. "Is he gone?"

He nodded and kicked at the spilled tray. "This is what made the noise." He didn't ask her why she had an untouched lobster salad sitting on the floor of her suite, but he wondered. Had she ordered it from room service before he'd called her about the pizza?

He dialed another number. "Lieutenant McQuade here.

You're the night guard? Check the area around the pool and grounds. We've had an intruder. Police are on their way." He pocketed his phone and turned to Victoria.

"You…come with me." He took her arm and guided her out the door and back down the hall to his suite, a little surprised that she wasn't peppering him with questions. Thankful, but surprised.

"Sit there." He pointed to the conference table as he turned the dead bolt on the door to the hall.

"Why? What are you going to do?"

And there she went with her questions. He didn't answer her. He just shot her a look. She got it because she sat down and clamped her mouth shut.

He headed into his sitting room, grabbed his hip holster and buckled it on. It was time to let people see his weapon. He sure as hell wasn't going to get caught without it again.

He grabbed his Stetson and returned to the conference room. Naturally Victoria wasn't sitting where he'd left her. She'd gone over to the sink and was washing her hands. She pressed wet fingers to her temples and under her eyes.

"I told you to stay put."

She jerked slightly and reached for a paper towel. "I felt grimy."

Right. He knew tears when he saw them. She was probably scared to death, and with good reason. He'd promised to protect her and he hadn't lived up to that promise. That was something else that was going to change. Right now.

She patted her cheeks and temples with the paper towel, her eyes on his weapon. "What are we going to do now?"

"What you're going to do is wait here until I get back."

"Wait? Alone? Oh, no, you don't. I'm not sitting in this room all by myself. I'm going with you."

"This is not negotiable, Vic. I'm in charge. I'm responsible. You do as I say."

"I don't see why—"

"Because there's a man out there who wants you dead!" he yelled.

Dammit, he never raised his voice. What was it about her that brought out the worst in him? "If I have to lock you in the bathroom I will."

Green sparks flashed in her eyes. "How can it be a good idea for me to stay here alone? Look what happened in my suite. I assume your bedroom has French doors, too."

"You'll stay here in the conference room. I don't have time to argue."

"And yet you are."

Brody clamped his jaw to stop an angry retort. "Just stay here and don't open the door to *anybody* but me. I'm locking you in." He turned on his heel, then turned back. "Do you know how to use a gun?"

She shook her head. "I've never even held one, but I'm sure I can point and shoot."

"Could you kill someone if your life was threatened?"

She looked at her hands. "Yes." She raised her head. "Yes." *She could.* He had no doubt.

Propping a boot on the coffee table, he retrieved the small semiautomatic from an ankle holster. "Will you promise me you won't shoot yourself?"

"Will the bullet go in the direction I point the barrel?"

He did his best not to smile as he flipped the gun and handed it to her handle first. "That lever is the safety. The gun won't fire with it on. Flip it with your thumb and squeeze the trigger and you'll blow a hole in whatever you're aiming at— even your foot."

He wondered if he was an idiot to give her a gun. But he only had two choices—take her with him or give her a means to protect herself.

"I've watched TV shows and movies. I don't rattle easily."

"It's not as easy as you think, shooting someone."

"Have you?"

Brody pushed his pants leg back down over his boot and reached for the doorknob. "I've got to get out of here. Who do you open the door for?"

"Nobody—except you." She set the gun down on the table, its barrel pointed toward the far wall. Her face was pale, but her fingers didn't shake and she had that determined tilt to her chin that he'd learned to believe.

"Good. I'm locking the dead bolt. I'll be back soon."

"Brody?"

He stopped on his way out the door.

"Be careful."

He stuck his hat on his head and touched the brim in a small salute. "Always am."

Victoria heard the steel bolt snick into place. She hadn't noticed that the rooms had double dead bolts operated by keys. She'd assumed the magnetic card was the only lock. While she looked at the keyhole on the inside of the door, it occurred to her that she couldn't get out through that door if she wanted to.

But what about the other doors—the French doors? She studied the layout of the conference room. She'd already noticed the three doors in the back wall. Those were the suites—like hers except that these were obviously designed for several people working together. She was certain that two of the doors led to the rooms of Brody's team.

She walked over and examined the doors. They all had

dead bolts, too. She tried each knob in turn, just to be sure they were locked.

Then she looked around. What if she had to go to the bathroom?

Oh, please, Victoria. "As if going to the bathroom is your biggest problem," she muttered. She sat with the gun on the table in front of her.

If someone else had a key, or if someone broke down the door, could she shoot them? She'd told Brody she could.

She took a long, shaky breath. Well, she'd better be ready to put a bullet into someone if she wanted to stay alive.

THE UNMISTAKABLE SOUND OF an electronic lock whirring woke Victoria. Her head snapped up and her hand closed around the gun before she even took a breath.

Calm down. It's Brody. It had to be. She was in the Rangers' conference suite at the country club. Who else would have a key?

Nobody—except the man who'd gotten into her apartment *twice* and into her suite at the country club. Nobody except the man who was trying to kill her.

She held the gun with both hands. With her right thumb she flicked the safety off. What had Brody said? *Squeeze the trigger and—*

The whirring stopped and started, stopped and started. She heard a muttered curse word. Then a key turning in the dead bolt sent her heart bouncing into her throat. She swallowed, wondering if she should say anything— even if she could.

Raising the gun a fraction of an inch, she slid her finger into the trigger guard. She hoped she didn't look as scared to death as she felt.

Could you kill someone if your life was threatened?

Brody's words echoed in her ears. If someone lunged at her, *could* she pull the trigger? She was about to find out.

The doorknob turned with excruciating slowness, like a scene in a grade B movie. Victoria straightened her arms.

A long arm in a white dress shirt with the sleeves rolled up pushed open the door. When the rest of him appeared around the door, Victoria knew she'd never seen him before.

"Why the hell is the dead bolt—"

"Stop right there!" she commanded.

"Holy crap!" The intruder froze. "Don't shoot, lady." His dark-lashed eyes were wide with shock as he slowly raised his hands. "You got me."

"Don't move a muscle," she said.

"Not moving a muscle. Get to the next part—who *are* you? I'm Hayes Keller, Texas Ranger. I'd show you my badge, but I left it in the car." He raised one hand toward his hat.

Victoria gripped the gun so tightly the barrel shook. "I said don't move."

"Whoa, lady. I don't like how you're holding that gun. Now, I'm not going to hurt you. I live here, at least temporarily. And judging by that gun you're holding, which belongs to Brody, I'd say you're either his guest or you've taken him captive. And since he's not sitting here hog-tied, I'm guessing it's the former. Mind telling me why my usually levelheaded lieutenant let you have a loaded weapon?"

Victoria shook her head to try to clear the haze from her mind. The guy was talking fast and her sleepy brain was listening slow. "Who did you say you are?"

"Name's Hayes Keller. Can I put my hands down? They're getting tired."

"No! I asked you a question."

"Yeah." His gaze narrowed for an instant, then he lowered

his hands and took a step inside. "I don't think you're going to shoot me. At least not on purpose. So why don't you lay the gun on the table and let's talk."

"Brody told me not to let anyone in except him."

"Right. Good plan. Except he didn't know I was coming in tonight." Hayes jerked a thumb toward the east. "Just drove in from Austin."

He sounded sincere. His ironic tone and devil-may-care attitude was too easy to be forced. She knew Brody had two men on his team. And he'd talked about Hayes. Maybe she *could* set the gun down.

"That's right, Annie Oakley. Just set it down."

She flipped the safety back on and put the gun down, but she didn't take her eyes off him.

"What the hell?"

"Damn!" Hayes jumped a foot in the air.

Victoria saw Brody behind him, and the breath she hadn't known she was holding whooshed out.

"You didn't tell me—" she started.

"You're not supposed to be here, Keller—"

"Crap, Brody. She could have shot my head clean off."

Everybody was talking at once, but Victoria managed to sort it all out. She clasped her hands and pushed her knuckles against her teeth.

Hayes gave Brody the five-second explanation for why he'd come in tonight. Brody gave Hayes the five-minute explanation of the break-in at Victoria's suite and why she was here with his spare gun.

She listened intently and never took her eyes off Brody. He was restless, pacing back and forth, grabbing a bottle of water from the refrigerator and downing it in one gulp, fiddling with his holster.

"Deason's got a roadblock set up, but so far the only person he's caught is Miles Landis. Landis had just parked here and was on his way to the bar for a nightcap before heading to the condos. At least that's his story. He doesn't look coolheaded enough to break and enter and then act like he's just out for a drink. I'm sure the perp hightailed it out before the police got here."

Brody sent a look Victoria's way. "You okay?" he asked belatedly.

She was tired and scared and a little intimidated by all the testosterone in the room. "Sure. I'm fine. I don't know if you had fun tonight, but I sure did. Everything from the pizza to the break-in to meeting…" She nodded toward Hayes, who took off his hat.

"Hayes," he said, affecting a little bow.

She glared at him, then turned her gaze back to Brody. "…to meeting *Hayes* when he just waltzed in using a key you told me nobody had."

"I didn't tell you that."

"Well, you implied it."

"Look, Vic. You're exhausted. You can sleep in my room and I'll sleep on the couch in the sitting room. That way you'll be safe and I'll know where you are."

"Here? You want me to stay here?" She looked from him to Hayes and back to him. "With the two of you? There's another one, too, isn't there? Three of you? No."

"Vic—"

"No, no, no." She shook her head. "Find me another suite. Isn't there one that doesn't open to the outside—or isn't full of men?"

"I'll show you to my room and Hayes will go get your clothes."

"Hey, leave me out of it. I'm on her side. Can't she stay somewhere else?"

Brody quelled him with a glance.

Hayes held up his hands. "Fine. Fine. Going to get the clothes." Brody handed him her card and he left the room.

Victoria crossed her arms and tried to cut Brody in half with a look. It didn't work. He didn't even wince.

"What did I tell you?" he said evenly. "I'm in charge. You listen to me. You're in my—in the Rangers' protective custody, and if I tell you you're sleeping in the same *bed* as me, that's what you'll do. Understood?"

Despite his words, which conjured up an image in Victoria's brain that melted her anger and heated her insides, she saw that he was really angry.

Black fire raged in his dark eyes. Something else did, too, or she thought it did. But it was probably a trick of the light. Either that or Brody McQuade took his job much more seriously than anyone she'd ever known. Because she saw a steely determination in him that could bring a professional wrestler to his knees.

She ought to be cringing. But for some weird reason, all his fierceness made her feel safe. "I apparently don't have any choice," she said grudgingly.

"That's right. You don't."

"Here you go." Hayes shouldered the door open. He was hauling a sheet that he'd obviously dumped everything into. "I think I got everything. Want this in your bedroom, Brody?"

Victoria looked at the makeshift sack. "Please tell me you didn't dump the food tray in there."

"I didn't dump the food tray in there."

"Put it in my bedroom." Brody nodded toward the middle door, then turned to her. "You can sort it out in the morning. Right now you need to get some sleep."

Hayes threw the sheet over his shoulder like a duffel bag, and Victoria winced at the sound of glass and plastic clanking together. He unlocked the door in the middle of the far wall.

"He has a key to your room?"

"They're all the same key. You can trust Hayes and Egan, just like you trust me."

"That much, eh?"

Brody frowned at her.

"Sorry. I'm getting loopy. I must be tired."

"Come on, then, I'll get you settled in."

Hayes came out minus the sheet, pointing with his thumb over his shoulder. "Your bedroom's kind of messy for a *girl*, Brody."

Brody shot him a look, then placed his hand on the small of her back and led her through the door into a small sitting room with French doors leading out to the pool.

"See. My room has the French doors out here. So you won't have to worry about someone breaking into the bedroom." He went into the bedroom ahead of her and grabbed up a towel and an undershirt and a pair of boxers from the floor.

"Sorry."

She looked around. The room wasn't luxurious—it was obviously designed for businessmen—but it was large enough for a king-size bed and a dresser. The bathroom door was open and she saw a spa tub and a walk-in shower. Dear heavens, a bath sounded good.

"Is this the only bathroom?" she asked.

"Yeah. There's one off the conference room, which I can use. No shower, though."

She stared at him helplessly.

"I'll use Egan's—or Hayes's." He looked at the floor. "Well, good night."

"Brody? Aren't you going to tell me what happened to the man who broke into my room?"

"You heard most of it. Basically he got away."

"Nothing? No fingerprints? No tire tracks?"

He shook his head. "We'll go over the area again in the morning, but I'm afraid he got away clean."

"So he's still out there and still wants me dead."

"Yeah, but you're here." He lifted a hand, then checked it before he touched her. "Safe."

Her heart skipped a beat. Probably because of the excitement and the danger and her exhaustion. "I hope you're right."

"I'll be just outside this door, on the sofa. You call out if you need me."

Victoria nodded.

Brody turned on his heel and walked through the sitting room and out into the conference room. She watched him—his strong, broad shoulders, his lean hips and sexy butt, the slight wave in the hair at his nape that made his otherwise straight back and neck look vulnerable.

Just as she was about to close the door to the bedroom, she heard Hayes.

"What the heck are you doing?" he asked. "What's the point of putting her in here? You don't think that's going to stop him, do you?"

"I think it'll draw him out. And when he tries to get to her, he'll fall right into our trap."

"Damn, Brody. You're using her as bait?"

"Keep your voice down."

Chapter Eight

Victoria couldn't breathe. Invisible hands closed around her throat and a soundless voice rasped in her ear. "He used you as bait, but I caught you." The hands squeezed tighter.

Victoria gasped. She flailed her arms, trying to fend off the faceless attacker. Her chest burned. Her throat hurt. She couldn't breathe.

Then she woke up.

It took her a couple of seconds to ground herself in reality. She was in Brody's bedroom. She was safe.

But her face was bathed in sweat, her mouth was dry and her body radiated heat. The tiny bedroom was closing in on her. She needed to get out of there.

To do that she'd have to go past Brody, who was asleep on the couch in his sitting room.

She tried to swallow, but her throat was too dry. Her heart fluttered in rising panic. Throwing on her kimono, she quietly opened the bedroom door.

The solar lights from the pool area seeped in around the lined curtains and bathed the sitting room in soft golden light. The *empty* sitting room. Her heart skipped a beat.

Brody wasn't there.

Settle down, she admonished herself. He was probably in the bathroom or had gotten up to get some water.

Victoria opened the suite door and stepped into the conference room. Cool air swirled around her. She took a long breath—and coughed.

"Vic?"

She jumped. *Brody.*

"You okay?"

He was standing at the sink, dressed in those truly sexy jeans and no shirt. Shadows planed his long, sleek muscles and the strong bones of his face.

Looking at him, she couldn't help but remember hearing him earlier, when he'd come into the sitting room. He'd tried to be quiet, but she'd woken up when the door closed.

She'd heard the rustle of clothes and the sound of boots hitting the floor, one at a time.

Finally he'd sunk onto the couch with a soft groan. It had taken her a long time to stop thinking about him lying there not thirty feet away in—what? Those jeans? Boxers? Nothing?

So now she knew the answer to that question.

"I just—" her hand flew to her throat "—just needed some water."

He opened the under-counter refrigerator, retrieved a bottle and loosened the cap. When he handed it to her his hand brushed hers and her heart fluttered again.

"Couldn't sleep?" His sleepy voice rumbled through her.

She shook her head. "I had a bad dream."

"About your attack?"

"And then the room started closing in." She walked over to the sitting area where she plopped down with her feet tucked under her.

She turned up the bottle and let the cool water slide over her aching throat. "What about you?"

He shrugged and gestured with the bottle in his hand. "Thirsty."

"I'm sure that couch is uncomfortable. I'm sorry for kicking you out of your bedroom."

"You're not kicking me out. I can sleep anywhere." He propped a hip on the high, overstuffed arm of the leather couch opposite her. "Now, tell me about your dream."

Victoria touched her throat. "It was nothing. I guess my throat was hurting, so I dreamed that he was choking me."

"Any specifics? Anything you haven't already remembered?"

"No." She took a long swallow of water. "He did tell me I was bait."

Brody winced. "Hayes shouldn't have said that."

Victoria's mouth curved up in a rueful smile. "It's true, though."

"I would never risk your life."

"I know that, but he's going to come after me, no matter what. I'm just glad I'm here with you."

Brody didn't answer. He finished his water and stood.

"Are you going back to bed?" Her eyes caught the light and sparkled like jade.

"I was. Do you need something?"

Her gaze faltered. "No, that's okay."

"Vic? Are you still spooked?"

"Could you just sit with me for a little while? Just a few minutes?"

Brody sat back down and rested his elbows on his knees. He didn't really want to sit here dressed in nothing but jeans while she sat across from him in that clingy kimono, but as much as he wanted to get away from her enticing presence, he couldn't refuse.

She sat there looking at her half-empty water bottle.

He studied her. Her hair was twisted up into a messy little knot at the back of her head, and strands of it had fallen around her face. It was soft and honey-colored, the kind of hair that made a man want to pull out whatever was holding it up and let it fall.

"Tell me about your parents."

"What?" She'd caught him totally off guard.

"You said Carlson was your foster brother."

"Right." Brody suddenly felt like his skin had been flayed off. "I also said it was a long, sad story. Too long. You need to go to sleep."

She looked at him, a small wrinkle between her brows. "I'd like to know."

He opened his mouth to refuse, but that would just make her more curious. And he had the definite feeling she wouldn't stop asking until she got her answer.

"Okay, here's the short version. My parents died when I was eleven. My sister was six. There were no close relatives, so we went into foster care. That's how I ended up with Carlson as a foster brother."

"Oh, Brody. Both your parents at the same time? What happened?"

And there he was. In the middle of a conversation he didn't want to have. He was not going to talk about his parents. He was not going to tell Victoria Kirkland anything else about his life. No useful purpose could be served.

He stood. "They died in a plane crash. Now—we both need to get some sleep."

"I HAVE TO GO IN to the office today. There's a partners' meeting, plus I have a brief due on Monday, and as I've already told you, my files are there." Victoria stood in the doorway of Brody's suite and glared at him.

He blew across the surface of his mug, then took a sip of coffee. He was in those ridiculously sexy jeans, but at least this morning he wore a T-shirt. It was faded green and read Habitat for Humanity. His hair was tousled, as if he'd tossed and turned all night.

She'd slept badly, too, after their brief midnight encounter. She hadn't had another nightmare, but it had taken her a long time to calm her mind enough to sleep. His matter-of-fact recitation of how he and his sister had ended up in foster care hadn't fooled her. His ironclad control telegraphed how much the deaths of his parents had hurt him. And now he'd lost his only sister. She'd cried for him.

"You should've brought your stuff home with you. Want some coffee?"

So much for feeling sorry for him. The annoyingly single-minded Texas Ranger was back.

She sighed in exasperation. "Brought my stuff? And why would I do that? Because I was *planning* to be attacked?"

He ignored her sarcasm. He turned his back and poured a mug of coffee. "You like sugar, right?"

His toned body made her mouth go dry.

She closed her eyes so she couldn't see his butt. "Not as much as you do."

The smell of coffee made her eyes fly open. He was holding the mug out toward her. "That's what I thought."

"Thank you. I need to go to the office." She flattened her mouth.

"Why didn't you tell me earlier?"

"Because I've been a little distracted. I'd forgotten about it until my PDA alarm rang this morning."

He nodded. "Okay. I have an appointment in Austin at ten o'clock. We'll swing by your office when we get back."

"Wait a minute. *You* have an appointment? What were you planning to do with me?"

"Take you with me."

"And when were you going to tell me that?"

Typically he didn't answer. He sipped his coffee and added another half-teaspoon of sugar to it.

"Well, I can't go with you. My meeting is at ten, too."

"Cancel it."

"Absolutely not. I can't do that. This is a twice-yearly international video-conference call. There are dozens of people involved. You change *your* appointment."

Brody blinked and she'd have sworn he winced. But before she could consider what had bothered him, he glared at her. She could practically see the wheels turning in his head. He was about to order her not to go.

"Look, Lieutenant. This is important. In fact, it's in my contract that I attend."

"Okay."

"You can't just— What?" Had he said okay? She looked at him suspiciously. "You did not just agree to let me go to my office alone. What's the catch?"

"No catch." Brody drained his mug, letting the undissolved sugar in the bottom slide into his mouth. Then he set it down and crossed his arms.

"I can't hold you prisoner. I know you have things you have to do. But you need to remember that there's someone out there who wants you dead. And I need to know where you are every minute. When I can, I'll send someone with you. When I can't, I want you in touch by phone."

He'd prefer to keep her glued to his side every minute. But today he had to sign some legal papers involving Kimmie's estate. He'd already put it off twice. He couldn't cancel again.

Egan was still in Austin, and Hayes had left before seven to get an early start scouring pawnshops all over the city for the humidor and the other missing items from the condos.

She searched his face for a few seconds, then hers turned pale. "I know you think whoever's doing this is the person who killed your sister. And that he's targeting me because he thinks I saw something. But I didn't. If I had, I'd have told the police long before now."

"We've been over this. We don't know what's in his head. And we can't afford to let down our guard for even a second. He could be a neighbor of yours, an employee either here or at the condos."

"Or a stranger."

"Or a stranger." He nodded and poured himself another mug of coffee.

"You really need to use less sugar."

Her voice was close. How quietly had she moved that he hadn't heard her approach? He looked down at her bare feet showing below her pale-green nightgown. She'd slung on the kimono, but as usual it was hanging open. All he had to do was raise his gaze to see the material clinging to her hipbones and that hint of a V that drove him nuts. A little farther up and he'd encounter her perfect breasts. He knew if he let his eyes linger there long enough for her to notice, he'd see their tips tighten with awareness.

And he wanted to see that more than anything in the world. But speaking of tightening, he had to get control of himself or she was going to know exactly what he was thinking. He grimaced as he stirred his coffee, but his brain wasn't ready to let go of the erotic image of her in her seemingly unending supply of slinky lingerie.

This was what hell must be like—or heaven. Doomed to an eternity of Victoria Kirkland parading around in lace and satin, torturing him with what he couldn't have.

"Brody?"

He tapped the spoon on the edge of the mug for a second or two until he decided it was safe to turn around without embarrassing himself.

"You said the attacker could be an employee at the condos or here at the country club."

"Yeah?"

"What if it's both?"

He stopped stirring. "Both? What do you mean, both?"

"I'm pretty sure there are a few employees I've seen working here and at the condos."

Both! Of course. "I'll be damned. Vic, you're a genius!" It made perfect sense! He'd talked to the employees about what they'd seen. But she was right. He needed to question the ones who worked both at Cantara Gardens and at the country club. Whoever was after Victoria had access to both.

He needed to get a list of every employee who used a key, instead of an access card, anyhow.

Even if the employees weren't involved, they could have noticed something he'd missed, since he was unfamiliar with the area.

"You don't have to sound so surprised. I do occasionally have a good idea."

He looked at his watch. "I've got to shower. I need to leave by eight-thirty. When are you leaving?"

"About the same time. I shouldn't be gone more than two or three hours. Four at the most. I was going to shop for some clothes, since my apartment is still off-limits, but I can do without that. I'll just wear my black pants every day."

Brody tried unsuccessfully to hide a smile. "I'm sure you can manage for a couple of days without a new outfit."

Her chin lifted a fraction. "I don't need a new outfit. I just need something to wear besides pajamas or shorts."

At least her pajamas covered more than those slinky night-gowns she'd worn the first two nights. "Here's what you're going to do. You go to your office and come straight back here, and you call me—" he counted off on his fingers as he spoke "—when you park the car, when you get to your office, when you're ready to leave, when you get into your car, and when you get back here. In fact, I want you to call if you change lanes on the interstate. Got it?"

"Sure. Call you every five minutes. Got it."

"It's not a joke, Vic."

"I know. But what about your appointment? I hate to call—"

"You call! There's nothing—" He stopped, thinking of his meeting with his lawyer about the disposition of Kimmie's estate, which brought out all the grief and anger of the past eight months. "There's nothing more important than your safety. If you call, I'll be there."

She nodded, and he saw the terror gathering like storm clouds in her eyes. "You're starting to scare me," she said.

"Good. Use that fear to sharpen your senses. You've got to be aware of everything that goes on around you. Don't let anyone surprise you or sneak up on you. Don't ignore anything that's even slightly out of the ordinary."

She wrapped her arms around herself. "Could you stop, please? I get it."

"I hope so, because it's the only thing that's going to keep you alive."

THAT CAR WAS STILL riding her tail. "Come on, pass me already."

Victoria turned her attention back to the Anderson Loop that wound above the city of San Antonio. Her hands tightened on the steering wheel. She didn't like this road. Didn't like knowing that a flimsy metal guardrail was all that stood between her car and a plunge down the side of a limestone bluff. Particularly didn't like that it was nearly dark.

She slowed down a little more. There was a relatively straight stretch of road ahead. "Okay, you're in such a darn hurry. Pass." She glanced in the mirror again, wishing the impatient driver would put on his headlights. It was that awful time between daylight and dark, when everything faded to a colorless gray and it was almost impossible to distinguish shadows.

Frustrated, she lowered her window and gestured for the car to go around her.

This was all Brody's fault. When she'd called to say she'd be leaving her office and heading back to the country club within an hour, he'd berated her about staying all day and commanded her to leave right away. He wanted her home before dark. If she'd waited like she'd wanted to, maybe the traffic pileup on the interstate wouldn't have forced her to take this detour.

A low-slung red Ferrari roared past, startling her. Maybe that was the problem. The Ferrari had been crowding the car behind her, forcing him to speed up.

Now the guy would pass.

Sure enough, he crept closer and closer. It took all her willpower not to speed up. She didn't like being tailgated. She set her jaw and waited for him to pull out and around, but he seemed content to ride her tail. Was he too chicken to pass?

Her cell phone rang. *Great.* She wasn't going to answer it at first—she didn't want to take a hand off the wheel. But if it was Brody and she didn't answer, he'd likely mobilize the entire Texas Ranger force.

She dug in her purse and finally came up with the phone. It was Brody.

"Where are you?"

"I'm on the way home, on the Anderson Loop. I told you…"

"What's the matter?"

The car had dropped back a few feet so she slowed down a little more. "Nothing. There was a massive accident on the interstate so I took the Anderson. I do *not* like driving up here."

"You should have called me. How long before you get here?"

"Maybe half an hour. Sooner if this car won't pass me. I'm going to have to speed up. I can't stand to have a car tailgating me."

"Tailgating? What kind of car is it?" Brody's voice rose.

"I don't know. Maybe a GM? Midsize, kind of medium or dark blue. It's hard to say in this light."

"Listen to me, Vic. Drive as fast as you dare. That road's not as dangerous as it looks. But be careful. Don't let him rattle you."

"No worries. I have you to do that."

"Vic, I told you, this is not a joke. Where are you? What was the last exit you saw?"

"I've passed Hollywood Park." She didn't like the urgent tone in Brody's voice. He was beginning to scare her.

"Okay. Take 1535 and drive straight to the police station. It's on Shavano Park on your right. Don't stop anywhere. If the guy follows you off that exit, call me. I'm heading over there now."

"Brody, you don't think it's the killer…" But Brody had hung up.

Victoria's apprehension rose exponentially. She looked in the rearview mirror. She couldn't see anything except the glare from the car's tinted windows.

Victoria set her phone in the passenger seat. Talking to Brody, hearing the innate assurance and confidence in his voice always made her feel better. But this time, he hadn't disguised his concern about the car following her. He'd sounded anxious, and that scared her to death.

A bump threw her head back.

Ouch. What was that? A rock? She glanced in the rearview mirror just in time to see the dark sedan speeding toward her. Instinctively she braced herself.

It happened again. Her head hit the headrest—hard.

Dear heavens, he was ramming her. Her cramped fingers gripped the steering wheel more tightly. She sped up, following Brody's instructions.

The car fell behind. Victoria blew out a shaky breath. She sat stiffly, holding on to the steering wheel for dear life. She drove as fast as she dared, looking for the turn onto 1535. She didn't drive this road enough to know how far she was from it, but she suspected it was almost to the end of the road. How much farther did she have to drive up here, suspended above the world?

A movement in her mirror caught her attention. The car was speeding toward her again. She floored the accelerator, her heart slamming against her chest, her sweat-slick palms slipping on the wheel. For some reason she was hyperaware of everything—the darkening sky, the guardrail, the sound of the car behind her.

She couldn't keep up this speed. She'd crash. Sweat broke out on her forehead and slithered down her back. She set her jaw and kept her tight grip on the wheel, afraid to let go even long enough to wipe her clammy hands on her pants.

The dark blue car loomed in her rearview mirror.

Objects are closer than they appear. Was that even possible? She didn't think the car could get any closer.

Then she heard the crunch of metal. Her head slammed backward. Hot panic ripped through her like an electric shock and stars danced in front of her eyes. She stomped on the accelerator again.

Brody!

Another crunch. Another jarring blow. This time the metallic shriek went on and on, echoing in her ears from behind her, in front of her—from everywhere.

And then all sound was gone and the world was spinning. Somewhere in the back of her rational brain, she knew it wasn't the world, it was her. But her eyes and her senses were feeding her brain mixed messages.

She gripped the steering wheel like a lifeline and fought for control, but nothing stopped the endless silent spinning. There was nothing to steer—her wheels weren't touching the ground.

The front of her car sideswiped the guardrail, throwing all her weight forward into the seat and shoulder belts. Metallic screeching filled her ears as the car slid sideways along the rail.

She saw nothing except streaks—the world flying by. It looked like a time-lapse shot of a car race—red and black and blue blurry stripes. She closed her eyes. Soon she'd be weightless—flying—falling—dying.

Another bump, another earsplitting screech, then nothing.

Vaguely, distantly, Victoria heard the sound of sirens. She forced her eyes open and tried to make sense of what she saw.

Her brain fought the truth. Dizziness and nausea engulfed her. She blinked again and again, but the reality didn't change. Relentlessly, cruelly, it taunted her with the truth laid out in front of her. She was looking down at the bottom of a cliff. The seat belt bit into her flesh. Her neck hurt. Echoes of screeching metal still filled her ears.

What she saw couldn't be real, could it?

She cut her eyes to the side, trying not to move, and saw a curled piece of galvanized metal. It looked like a used sardine-can lid. It was the guardrail.

Suddenly, whatever part of her brain controlled her balance rebelled at what her eyes saw. Her world began to spin again, and nausea burned in her throat. She closed her eyes, but it didn't help.

Her car was tipped precariously over the edge of a precipice and every few seconds it creaked and teetered.

Her throat ached with the need to scream. Her stomach clenched with panic. She dared not move, hardly dared to breathe. One deep breath, one tiny shift in position could upset the tenuous balance and send her crashing dozens of feet to the ground.

Somewhere behind her a car's engine roared and a muffled yell rang out. It was him! The man who'd forced her off the road. He was coming to finish her off.

She gasped, and pain sliced through her chest. Dear heavens, that hurt! She carefully tested her arms and legs by moving them slightly.

More pain.

She held her breath as she did a mental inventory. Head—pounding. Chest—shrieking pain with each breath. Arms and legs—tingling.

She tentatively peeked down at herself. She didn't see any blood. That was good. Wasn't it?

Or was it? No blood didn't mean no injuries. Her tummy and chest ached. Her head pounded, and all she could think about was that if her car tilted another inch, she'd plunge to her death without seeing Brody again.

She became aware of more noise. Suddenly the dark world around her was awash with light. She squinted. The light hurt her eyes.

More shouts and a loud roar that sounded bigger than a car engine.

Victoria tried to turn her head and look behind her, but when she did metal screeched in protest and she felt her world tilt a little more off center.

Brody! "Get Brody," she screamed, but her brain knew that the sound coming out of her mouth was nothing more than a whisper.

"Hang on, lady! Don't move!"

She lifted her head. Had someone said something to her? A trickle of warmth tickled her cheek. She peeled her fingers off the wheel and touched the itchy place.

Blood. It was blood. She *was* injured. Fear sliced through her. Was it better to plunge down a mountain or bleed to death? Either way, she wasn't going to make it.

Her chin dropped to her chest. She was so tired. Maybe she'd just close her eyes and rest for a few moments.

"Ma'am? Miss Kirkland? Can you hear me? Don't move, just speak."

"I can hear you," she whispered. "Who are you? Are you here to kill me?"

"No, ma'am."

Her head ached and it hurt her chest to talk. If he wasn't going to kill her, what was he doing here?

"Go away." If she took a nap, surely Brody would be there when she woke up. "I'm waiting for Brody."

"Ma'am, can you tell me who you are?"

"Of course I can."

"Ma'am?"

Why was he bothering her? "Call Brody," she said drowsily.

"First tell me your name." His voice was young, very young.

She lifted her head and frowned. Her name. "Vic. It's Victoria."

"That's good. Victoria what?"

"Um…Kirkland. Who are you?"

"I'm one of the EMTs, Ms. Kirkland. Are you hurt anywhere? Bleeding?"

"Just my head."

"Nothing else? Your legs? Can you feel them? Can you wiggle your toes?"

"Yes, I already checked. But my chest hurts. Can you help me out of here?"

"Hold on, ma'am. Don't move just yet. We need you to wait just a little while. We need to make sure the car is steady before we extract you. So can you sit still for me? Help me keep the car steady?"

"Steady. Slow and steady wins the race."

"That's right. Now we're going to attach a chain to the frame of your car. The car will probably move, but don't worry. We'll have you. You'll be okay. And stay still!"

The end of his sentence was drowned out by the sudden, discordant sound of metal against metal.

"No!" she screamed. "No!" The ground below her and the darkening sky above dipped and soared. She braced herself. Any second the car would tilt forward and plunge down the cliff.

"Ms. Kirkland?" a different voice said. "Are you awake?"

"Yes," she mumbled. "The car's going over, isn't it?"

"Not right now. I'm Pete Chaney, Ms. Kirkland. I'm the fire chief. We've got the chain around your rear axle, and I need you to help me with something."

"All you guys need my help, don't you?"

Victoria heard Pete Chaney chuckle, and she wondered what was so funny.

"Yes, ma'am. We can't do it without you. Now, I've got a fireman here who needs to put a belt around you."

Victoria tried to open her eyes, but the lights were bright and she was getting really tired. "I've got a belt around me. I always wear my seat belt."

The voice got closer. It was a deep voice, strong. Not as deep or strong as Brody's, but close. "Here's the fireman. His name's Dave."

"Hi, Victoria. People call you Vicky?"

"No. People call me Victoria." She smiled. "Brody calls me Vic."

"Okay then, Victoria. I need to cut your seat belt so it doesn't get in our way."

"I need my seat belt."

"I'm going to give you a better one, okay? It slips under your arms and over your shoulders."

"Like yours?"

"Exactly like mine. We want to make sure we hang on to you. I promise it will only take a minute."

Victoria felt his warm hands on her. "Are you getting into the car?"

"No." His voice sounded a little strained. "I've got to do this without touching the car, and you need to stay perfectly still. Let me move your arms, okay? You just go limp."

He touched her left arm. "Don't stiffen up, Victoria. We're almost done."

The next thing Victoria knew, the man was gone and the fire chief was talking to her again.

"Hi, Ms. Kirkland. You're all harnessed up. Now comes the scary part. We're going to haul the car up. It's going to be loud and really scary, so I need you to be very brave. Can you do that?"

"Where's Brody? Did somebody call him?"

"Lieutenant McQuade called us. He's on his way." Chaney turned.

"Where are you going? You're not leaving me here, are you?"

"No, ma'am. I'm just going to wait over there while my guys do their job. It'll just be a couple of minutes. Remember, we've got a big chain around your car and a harness around you. If everything goes perfectly, you and the car will be back on solid ground in no time, safe and sound."

Victoria nodded, praying he was right, praying that her car wouldn't break apart, praying Brody would hurry up and get there.

She heard a monstrous engine roar. Less than a second later, the bottom fell out of her world.

The car plunged forward, throwing her back against the seat and slamming her head against the headrest.

The fireman had lied to her. She was going to die.

Chapter Nine

The first thing Brody saw was Victoria's car slipping over the precipice. The noise was deafening as the chain attached to her rear axle creaked and strained. The rescue vehicle's engine roared as it worked to pull the Lexus backward, away from the cliff.

Sick horror closed Brody's throat. Was she still in there?

He leaped out of his Jeep and barreled through the circle of police and fire vehicles.

Dear God, hold on to her, he prayed.

At that instant a metallic clang echoed through the air. The massive chain snapped like a rubber band. It catapulted backward, missing one of the firemen by inches.

The Lexus teetered on the edge of the precipice, grating against the shredded guardrail.

"Vic! No!" His voice broke. He hurtled toward the car as panic and desperation burned through him. *You can't die. Not you, too.*

Brody slammed into a rock—that's what it felt like. Pete Chaney grabbed him just as the shriek of metal against metal split the air and Victoria's Lexus tipped forward and slid over the edge of the limestone bluff.

Brody froze, unspeakable pain searing every cell of his body. A raw, wordless cry ripped past his throat. Then he shoved Chaney, doubling his fists. "Let go of me! Bastard!"

"McQuade, she's not in there!"

The fire chief's voice echoed in his brain but the words made no sense. He broke Chaney's grip and stumbled.

"She's safe!" Chaney shouted.

Safe? Safe. It took a second for the word to make sense. He whirled around, his stomach churning with adrenaline. "What? Where?"

"Over there. They're putting her in the ambulance now. We extracted her through the driver's window."

Brody's tense muscles shivered in relief. His eyes stung. His throat spasmed. He covered the distance to the ambulance in two long strides.

"Hold it!" he croaked.

They stopped.

He saw a small shape under a sheet. "Vic?"

One of the EMTs looked up. "Are you Lieutenant McQuade?"

"Yes," he snapped, as he swiped a hand over his damp face, a hand that shook. "Texas Ranger. Victoria Kirkland is in our protective custody. I need to see her."

"We're taking her to County General. You can ride with her if you like."

Brody glanced over at his vehicle.

Chaney walked up beside him. "I can have someone take your car in for you."

Brody nodded, and climbed into the ambulance beside Vic's gurney. He met Chaney's eye. "Chief, I'm—"

Chaney touched the brim of his hat. "Don't mention it, Lieutenant. Just doing our job." As Chaney pushed the ambulance door closed, Brody nodded his head in thanks, then turned his attention back to Victoria.

Her eyes were closed and her mouth and nose were covered by an oxygen mask.

His heart leaped into his throat and lodged there. She looked so small and vulnerable. So breakable. He wanted to cradle her in his arms and promise her that nothing bad would ever happen to her again. But that would be a lie and Rangers didn't lie.

As the ambulance started up, Brody dug his cell phone out of his pants pocket, dismayed to notice that his fingers still shook. He pressed a familiar number.

"I need you back here."

"Dammit, Brody. Can't you take care of anything yourself?"

Brody knew Egan was just being his usual cranky self. He also knew he was joking, but Brody didn't have time for it. "Egan, listen to me."

His friend stopped grousing. "What's the matter?"

"Vic's car was forced off the road. She almost went over. I'm going to the hospital with her. I want you to process her car. If there's one speck of paint on it that doesn't belong, I want it."

"Crap! She okay?"

Brody looked at her. The delicate skin around her eyes looked bruised. Her skin seemed stretched too tightly across her cheekbones. And her hands were clenched into fists.

"Brody?"

"I don't know. I hope so."

Egan was silent for a fraction of a second. "What about you?"

"What about me?" He heard the edge to his voice.

"Yeah, well…nothing. I'll be there in a couple of hours."

"Make it one, Caldwell."

"You got it."

Brody pocketed his phone. The EMT sitting beside the gurney gently removed the oxygen mask from Victoria's face. When he did her eyes fluttered open.

Brody took her hand in his. He tenderly opened her fist, then ran his thumb across the half-circle imprints of fingernails on her palm.

"Br-Brody?"

"Hey, Vic. You had an adventure, but you're okay." He had a sudden, overwhelming urge to clear his throat.

"Where am I?"

"In an ambulance. We're taking you to the hospital, to get you checked out. How're you feeling?"

Her green eyes flashed with panic. "He ran me off…off the road. I couldn't get away. I couldn't make the car go fast enough."

"It's okay, Vic." Brody squeezed her hand. "You're safe now."

Her fingers squeezed his weakly. "I thought I was going to die. I was afraid you wouldn't come."

He lifted her hand and kissed her knuckles. "I swear on everything that's holy, Vic, I will always be there for you." Even as he said it, he knew he was lying.

It was a promise he couldn't make good on. He was a Texas Ranger and she was…she was Victoria Kirkland. After this case was over, he had no reason to ever see her again.

But Vic's pale face lit up and a little smile curled her lips. "Always," she whispered.

Brody put her hand down on top of the sheet that covered her. He patted it awkwardly. "You're safe. And I promise we'll find whoever did this. Could you see anything?"

Her gaze never left his. She shook her head. "The car was dark, maybe blue. The windows were tinted."

She closed her eyes and tried to moisten her dry lips. The EMT took her blood pressure and checked her pulse.

Then her fingers tightened convulsively around the sheet. "Brody?"

"Yeah?"

She opened her eyes and he saw that they glittered with dampness. "I'm so sorry. I swore I was going to be brave."

"You were. You are." He took a deep breath. "I'm the one who should apologize. I never should have let you out of my sight."

BACK AT THE COUNTRY club, Brody stopped the car and ran around to the passenger side. Victoria already had the door open.

"Hang on," he said. "I'll help you."

"Brody, I can walk. I'm not hurt." She wasn't sure she liked him like this—hovering, worried, acting as if he thought she'd break.

"Yeah? Those stitches above your right eye say otherwise."

She swung her legs out and started to stand, but pain from the massive bruise that ran from her left shoulder to her right hip surprised her. She gasped and tumbled back into the seat.

"See? There was a reason they brought you out to the car in a wheelchair."

"Right. The usual reason. They don't want a patient to fall on their way out of a hospital. Big lawsuit. Big money." She tried the standing-up thing again. But before she even managed to get upright, Brody was there, his arm around her waist.

"Spoken like an attorney," he murmured close to her ear.

A thrill slashed through her, weakening her knees. She was still spooked by her brush with death, but apparently Brody had the power to wipe the terror from her mind and replace it with lust. No, not lust.

It wasn't lust. It was probably gratitude and relief at being rescued.

"You don't have to help me."

"Indulge me," he said, his low voice rumbling through her. He held on to her and guided her up the steps and into the main reception room of the country club.

"I can walk by myself."

"You're groggy. The doctor gave you a tranquilizer."

"I don't remember taking anything."

"It was while you were in the ambulance."

Brody unlocked the door to the conference complex and guided her inside. He took her straight back to his suite and into his bedroom. "Can you change clothes by yourself?"

"Of course I can. You're acting as if I'd broken something."

"Vic, you almost plunged over a cliff. That drop would have killed you. You have a right to be scared and hurt. You have a right to depend on someone else. The doctor told me that between your seat belt and the rescue harness you've got a bruise the size of Oklahoma from your shoulder to your hip."

His gaze slid down her torso like healing fingers, leaving her skin sensitized and hot. Then his eyes snapped to her face.

Could he feel her response to him? She blinked and looked down at her hands, which were clasped in front of her.

All she wanted was to strip off her sweaty, wrinkled clothes and climb into bed. To feel the cool sheets against her burning body. To fall asleep feeling safe and protected.

She closed her eyes and took a deep breath. Brody's rain-fresh scent floated past her nostrils, weakening her knees.

"Whoa," Brody said, and suddenly she was enveloped in his strong arms, shielded against his broad chest. She felt the strong, steady beat of his heart against her palm.

"Vic, you're asleep on your feet. Let me get you into bed."

As he said it, she realized that was exactly what she wanted—for Brody to take her to bed. It had been over a year since her fiancé had died. She'd hardly dated—she certainly hadn't slept with anyone.

But Brody was all wrong for her. No, she was all wrong for him. She was too tired to think, but she knew somebody was all wrong for somebody.

"I think I need a bath," she murmured. "I'm filthy."

She felt a soft rumbling in his chest. It almost pushed aside the sleepy haze that enveloped her. Was Brody McQuade laughing?

"Yeah, you're all stinky," he muttered.

"Just point me to the bathroom and I'll be fine."

"There's no way I'm letting you get into that tub by yourself."

Victoria smiled at his choice of words. "You're going to get in with me?"

He turned red.

The sight of his cheeks blazing with color wiped a lot of the drowsiness from Victoria's brain.

"No," he snapped. "I'm going to sit you down on the side of the tub and give you what my foster mother used to call a spit bath."

He wrapped an arm around her waist and guided her into

the bathroom and sat her down on the wide edge of the spa tub. Then he started unbuttoning her blouse. His fingers, so much larger than hers, fumbled with the tiny pearl buttons.

"I'll do it," she said. "Just run some hot water. There are washcloths on the back of the toilet."

"I know. This is my room, remember?"

Brody set the stopper and ran hot water into the lavatory. He immersed a soft, white washcloth and squeezed it out, then lathered it with a miniature bar of glycerin soap. When he turned around, Vic had shed her blouse and pants. She sat on the edge of the tub in nothing but her bra and panties, and not much of them.

An ugly red-and-purple bruise ran from her left shoulder down across her midsection to her right hip. There were smaller matching blotches on her shoulders and upper arms.

His imagination fed him a horrifying image—Victoria, jerked like a rag doll through the window of her Lexus as the vehicle balanced crazily on the edge of the limestone cliff.

He cursed, lengthily and inventively.

Victoria's eyes widened and she spread a hand across her chest.

He pushed her hands aside and brushed the tips of his fingers over her damaged skin. "Dammit. This is my fault. I am so sorry, Vic. I didn't protect you."

She put a finger against his lips, and it was all he could do not to pull her to him and kiss every bruised millimeter of her body.

"Don't, Brody," she said. "You can't be everywhere. You warned me to be careful, and you told me to come straight home. It was my fault. I stayed and signed papers."

Would she have been safe if she'd followed his instructions? He'd like to believe she would have, but he had a sick feeling that whoever was after her was becoming bolder—or more desperate. Obviously the driver of the dark car had followed her. Had he waited all day for her to leave?

But tonight wasn't the time to remind her of how close she'd come to death.

Brody squeezed out the washcloth. Carefully, doing his best to avoid touching any intimate area, he washed her. From her dust- and tear-streaked face, down her delicately curved neck, across her bruised shoulders and down her arms, back to the tops of her breasts and her tummy, and the length of her thighs, the curve of her calves and the turn of her ankles and feet.

By the time he'd finished, he'd broken every last promise he'd made to himself. He'd touched the tops of her breasts and seen them tighten under the flimsy fabric of her bra. He'd seen—hell, he'd *lingered* on—the V formed by her pale, lacy panties. He'd run his hand, covered only by the square of terry cloth, up her inner thighs and nearly lost it when he saw her thigh muscles contract in response to his touch.

He'd ended up sporting a painful, throbbing hard-on there was no way in hell he could disguise. But to be fair, he'd been doomed from the start. When it came to Victoria, there wasn't a millimeter of skin that wasn't sexy.

"Okay," he croaked, tossing the cloth into the lavatory and standing. "I hope you feel better…" He left the rest of the sentence unsaid. There was no doubt in his mind that she knew the state he was in. But if she didn't say anything, he could escape with at least a smidgen of his dignity still intact.

He headed for the door. "I'll let you change clothes, and then you can go to bed."

Victoria had never been treated so gently, so reverently, in her life. It was that unbearable tenderness that Brody only exhibited when they were alone.

He'd made love to her body with that washcloth, and all her aches and fears had melted away in a sensual awareness of the thing between them. The thing that breathed dragon's fire through her down to the center of her sexuality.

She reached out and caught his arm.

He turned.

"Brody, don't leave."

He opened his mouth to protest, but she stopped him. She stood on tiptoe and kissed the side of his neck.

He ducked his head for an instant, then put his hand around the nape of her neck and kissed her forehead—not a quick good-night-sleep-well kiss.

His lips lingered on her skin like a lover's, and their touch swept through her like a whirlwind. She couldn't suppress a tiny moan. She lifted her hand and slid her fingers through his collar-length hair.

He raised his head, meeting her gaze with a questioning look. Then he lowered his mouth to hers. His lips and tongue explored hers thoroughly, intimately, in an imitation of love-making that stoked the fire he'd ignited.

Feeling Brody's arms enveloping her, his chest rising and falling with his rapid, steady breaths, energized her and tit-illated her.

For a few seconds he stood there, his nose pressed into her hair, one hand cradling the back of her head. She felt his erection pressing insistently, declaring his need for her.

She doubled her fists, catching and wrinkling his shirt. "Brody?" she whispered.

He lifted his head. "Vic..."

"Do *not* tell me not to get the wrong idea," she said. "I don't have the wrong idea. I have the *right* idea, and I *know* you do too." She ground her pelvis against his erection in case he had any doubt whatsoever about just exactly what she meant.

He tensed. "This is impossible. I can't do it."

"I'm pretty sure it's not impossible." She smiled at him.

He grabbed her upper arms and set her away from him. "I can't hide how much you turn me on, but I can't give in to it. You're in my protective custody. I can't take advantage of that."

"You've never once told anyone I was in *your* custody. You've always said the *Rangers'* protective custody."

"It's no different."

Victoria nodded. "You must have thought something would happen. Otherwise why make the distinction?"

He shrugged and looked away. "I needed everyone to understand that Egan and Hayes were just as responsible for you as I am."

"Brody..." She lifted her head and stood on tiptoe again. For an instant he strained away, trying to resist. But finally he bent his head so her mouth was near his ear. "Why do you call me *Vic?* Another attempt to distance yourself from me?"

His head snapped up. "Distance? No." He sounded genuinely bewildered.

"Then why?"

"I don't know. It fits."

She reached up to put her arms around his neck, and her sore muscles screamed in protest. She bit her lip.

"What's wrong?" Brody's brows drew down. "It's your shoulder, isn't it? See, you're too sore. I need to put you to bed."

She touched his mouth. "No. Don't put me to bed. *Take* me to bed."

"This is a big mistake," he muttered.

"I promise it isn't," she whispered back.

"You can't promise that. You don't understand all the ramifications."

"Of course I do. Want me to draw up a disclaimer?"

Irritation and something else flashed in his eyes and he took a step backward.

Victoria's stomach sank to the floor. She'd lost him with that last remark. It was probably for the best. He was right.

He'd be violating the code of any lawman, especially a Texas Ranger. Even though she'd only known him for three days, she knew upholding that honor was the cornerstone of his life.

"I'm sorry, Brody. I appreciate everything you've done. I didn't mean to make light of it—or of you." To her chagrin her voice broke on those last words. Her throat suddenly felt clogged with tears. She was going to cry.

Damn. Not in front of him. She turned away.

"Hey." He caught her arm. "Are you okay?"

She nodded, swallowing hard and blinking.

He stepped in front of her. "You're crying."

"No, I'm not." She wouldn't look at him. She wasn't one of those delicate, lovely, movie-star criers. When she cried her eyes got red immediately, her nose ran, and her cheeks grew blotchy. It wasn't a pretty sight. She took a deep breath.

"But I am tired." Good. Her voice was steady—sort of.

"Vic, it's okay to cry. You've been through a lot these past few days. Especially today."

"I don't cry." There went her nose. She sniffled and looked around for a tissue, but her eyes were growing blurry.

Brody stuck a handkerchief in her hand. She took it gratefully and blew her nose and wiped her eyes. "I'm sorry," she said with a short laugh. "I must have been more shaken by the accident than I thought I was."

Without speaking, Brody pulled her into his arms and cradled the back of her head. "Sure you were. And it was no accident."

Victoria's shoulders tightened at his words. She nodded against his shirt. "I know. Do you think you can find him?"

"I've already got Egan on it. He's processing your car. If the other car even grazed it, we'll get a paint sample that we can compare to the one on Caroline's car."

Victoria looked up at him and caught an odd expression on his face. His velvety black eyes searched hers. She just stood there, mesmerized, as he slowly lowered his head and pressed a kiss to her forehead.

It was a comforting kiss. A polite kiss. Certainly not the kiss of a lover— not this time. And yet it sent a sexual thrill through her. She slipped her arms around his waist and moved closer. The feel of him growing harder against her gave her courage to throw aside her inhibitions and take what she wanted.

She ought to respect his position, ought to accept that he didn't want to be distracted by sex. She ought to consider how angry he was going to be later if she succeeded in urging him to give in. But her body was alive with need—not just sexual. She needed his strength and craved the comfort of being surrounded by him, filled by him.

She kissed the side of his neck again and slid her palms up his back, feeling his hard planed muscles. Her pulse raced. She didn't know if it was from fear or excitement.

He pulled away.

"Brody, don't."

"Don't what?" he muttered. "Don't listen to my conscience? Don't remind myself that I'm a Texas Ranger and you're under my protection? Don't stop this before it goes too far?"

She put her fingers over his mouth. "Shh." Then she rose on tiptoe to kiss his mouth.

He lifted his head and put his hands on her shoulders. She braced herself, expecting him to push her away.

He thought about it—she could tell from the tensing of his forearms and the determination in his face. But instead of setting her aside and walking out, he held on to her shoulders and lowered his mouth to hers.

Victoria's insides went liquid and hot as he deepened the kiss and urged her mouth open with his tongue. She'd never experienced anything like his kiss. Unlike the last time he'd kissed her, he didn't stop and turn away. He kept going.

He stole her breath away with his firm, demanding mouth, his hot, delectable tongue, and the unmistakable promise of his erection pressing urgently against her as he pulled her into his arms.

"God help me," he whispered, his breath warming her lips. "Because obviously you're not going to."

Chapter Ten

Victoria could tell by the hardening of Brody's jaw that he was struggling with his conscience, his sense of duty and honor.

Part of her wanted his Ranger side to win. At least then she wouldn't be saddled with the guilt of compromising his principles. If he didn't stop himself, she knew she wasn't going to stop him. She couldn't. She wanted him too badly.

He flipped off the light and quickly shed his clothes.

When she saw his naked body backlit by the bathroom light, she had to suppress a gasp. He was less bulky than he looked in clothes, lean and toned and sexier than she'd imagined.

His long, sleek body was as perfectly toned as a swimmer's. The muscles of his arms and legs were smooth and well-defined, covered by golden skin that was paler on his torso and thighs.

He didn't waste time. He slid into bed beside her and pulled her close. She ran her fingers up his arms, touching his rock-hard biceps. "You're so beautiful," she whispered.

"Hey." He chuckled. "That's my line."

She shifted so her thighs rubbed against his. His erection pulsed against her belly and she gasped.

He froze. "Are you okay?"

"Yes." She sighed. "I just can't believe how wonderful, how beautiful you feel." She touched him.

He groaned quietly and pushed her hand away. "Don't. You don't know how close I am…"

She caught his hand and pressed it against her belly. "I know how close I am."

He kissed her and spread his fingers on her rounded belly, then slid his palm up her waist to her breasts. He undid the front clasp of her bra, tossing it aside, then he touched each breast, tracing its shape with his fingers, then dipping his head and drawing the puckered nipple into his mouth. He suckled on it until it stood taut and fiery red with sensation.

Victoria felt the gentleness of his touch as he skimmed her bruised flesh. He was so sweet, his fingers so tender and gentle—too gentle.

"I'm not made of porcelain, Brody. I won't break."

"But look at you," he growled. "Look at your skin. I don't want to hurt you."

"Listen to me, Lieutenant." Victoria put her lips on his and spoke against his mouth. "I'll be ten times as sore tomorrow morning, so please don't make me wake up frustrated, too."

He raised his head, his eyes as dark and bottomless as a pot of bitter chocolate. "You need to stop me."

In answer, Victoria wrapped her fingers around him and squeezed, until he groaned with pleasure.

"Vic!" His buttocks tightened and he strained toward her. "Be careful!"

Victoria bent her head and touched the tip of her tongue to his flat nipple, feeling it pebble under her mouth. She teased it with her teeth, then bent farther and ran her tongue along the hard ridges of his abdomen, then she moved lower.

"Ah, Vic, don't. If you keep that up, it'll be all over."

He grabbed her arms and pulled her to him, taking her mouth in a deep, erotic kiss. Then he set her back against the stack of pillows at the headboard and moved in front of her on his knees.

"What are you doing?" she panted.

"I don't intend to cause you any pain, just pleasure."

"Thank you," she whispered as he peeled her bikini panties down and off, then spread her legs and settled her so that her legs draped over his thighs.

Then he touched her, caressing and massaging the nub at the center of her being until she was moaning with pleasure and need. She felt liquid flow, felt her own slickness as he probed with his fingers, searching for the center of all her sensation.

And when he found it, she arched and curled as he gave her release. Then he wrapped his arms around her and kissed her.

Just when she thought she was drained of all sensation, he pushed into her, opening her more fully than she'd ever been opened, pushing more deeply than she thought possible, touching a point of ecstasy that no one had ever uncovered before.

He flattened his palm on her belly and slowly slid his hand downward until it pressed on her mound. She was boneless, completely at his mercy. He continued to move inside her as his fingers brought her to another, higher pinnacle of pleasure.

She moaned as her body strained toward the two equally erotic sensations—his erection pulsing inside her and his fingers driving her crazy. "Brody, please…"

But he didn't stop. He caressed and probed until her climax took her.

He threw his head back and growled as he thrust deeply into her. She caught his rhythm and met each stroke, taking all that he gave her until he hit yet another magical point.

She lost control as he found his own release. He pushed into her hard, again and again, intensifying her ecstasy.

Finally, when Victoria didn't think she had the energy to breathe, much less move, Brody pulled her into his arms and cradled her head against his shoulder. He ran his fingers up and down her curved spine and pressed his cheek against her hair.

"Vic, you okay?"

She nodded against the silk-over-steel smoothness of his skin. It took her a minute to find her voice.

"I'm fine." There was no way she could tell him just how fine she was. Brody McQuade had taken her further than she'd ever been before. He was strong and forceful, yet somehow gentler than any man she'd ever been with. The combination was a huge turn-on.

He eased off her and turned to lean back against the pillows. She laid her head on his shoulder again.

"You call me Vic," she murmured. "I've never had a nickname before. Nobody ever called me Vicky or Tory or anything like that. Not even my mother. Well, my grandpa called me Toto when I was little."

A soft chuckle rumbled in his chest, and he kissed her on the nose. "Go to sleep," he whispered. "You're half there already."

He slid his arm out from under her head, sat up and threw the covers aside.

"Where are you going?"

"I've got a few things I need to recheck, and I need to make arrangements to interview all our major suspects, see if they have an alibi for this—that is, yesterday—evening."

By the time he finished the sentence, his voice had turned harsh, and he didn't look at her.

"Brody? Are we okay?"

He didn't move for a moment, then finally he raised his gaze to hers. His dark eyes were still soft, but as she watched, they turned stone cold.

She sat up, pulling the sheet with her to cover her breasts. "Brody?"

"I don't know, Vic," he said, shaking his head. "I just don't know."

BRODY PULLED ON PANTS and left the bedroom. He pushed his fingers through his hair, grimacing. What the hell was he going to do now?

His pulse was still racing and his body was still tingling with the adrenaline rush of climax. The thought of Vic, languid and supple in his arms, her green eyes shining, sent a current of renewed lust rippling through him.

Calling himself some very rude names, he stalked across the small sitting room. He needed a bottle of cold water— maybe to drink, maybe to douse his head with.

He jerked open the door to the conference room and nearly ran smack into Egan.

"Whoa, Brody."

Great. He could hope Egan wouldn't pick up on what he'd been doing, but in his gut he knew his fellow Ranger was too sharp to miss it. He pushed past him with an aggressiveness that wasn't warranted.

"Hey!"

Egan grabbed his arm, but Brody shrugged him off and kept going. When he straightened from grabbing a bottle of water out of the refrigerator, the surly Ranger sergeant was right there.

"What's going on? You're throwing your weight around like a pissed-off bear."

Brody glared at him and pushed past him again. He took a big swig of water and wiped his face. The water cooled him down—a little. But dammit, the last thing he needed right now was Egan crawling his butt.

He turned and did what he did best. Turned a poor defense into a good offense. "What the hell are you doing here?"

Egan frowned. "You called and ordered me back here just a few hours ago. What the hell's wrong with..." Then his face changed.

His brows shot up and his mouth dropped open in shock. After a couple of grueling seconds of stunned silence, Egan glanced back at the door to Brody's suite.

Brody took another gulp of water and steeled himself for the explosion. It didn't take long.

"Son of a— Is Victoria in there? What the hell have you done?" Egan got in his face. "Are you out of your ever-loving mind?"

"Take a step back, Caldwell."

"Yeah. You should've taken that advice yourself." Egan threw up his hands. "I can't believe...I'd never have thought...damn!"

Egan was speechless. If Brody had been in the mood, his friend's reaction might have been funny. But Brody was *not* in the mood.

"What are you going to do now?"

Brody shrugged and then finished his water. He stalked across the room and threw the empty bottle into the trash can. Hell if he knew.

He'd screwed up royally.

"Where was your head?" Egan slapped the mahogany table with his palm. "Don't answer that. I know where it was."

Brody took a deep breath and hoped what he was about to do wasn't insane. If it was, he was sure Egan would let him know. "Nothing's going to change. Tonight was a…an aberration. She could have died. She was scared."

"So you thought you'd give her the *cure?*"

Anger set sparks exploding in front of Brody's eyes. He made a fist and took a step forward, but Egan just lifted his chin.

"Really?" Egan growled. "You're actually going to try that?"

Brody flexed his fingers and cursed. "It won't happen again. She's still in my protective custody. And, Caldwell, if you even *think* about this when you see her…well, just don't."

"Don't worry. I won't embarrass *her.*"

Egan met his gaze and Brody saw a look of disdain on his face. He felt like the world's biggest heel. He crossed his arms and waited to hear what else Egan had to say.

"Wow, Brody." The younger man looked stunned. He shook his head. "You're the last man on earth I'd have believed would get involved with a victim. Ever since we were kids, I thought you were a damned *saint.* But you're just as horny and lowdown as the rest of us."

Brody winced internally. He didn't need Egan to tell him what a jerk he was. If Egan was shocked by his actions, Brody himself was staggered—and outraged. This case was the most important one he'd ever worked. It was for Kimmie.

Ah, hell. That must be the problem. His feelings were too close to the surface. The case was too personal. Well, he'd just have to work that much harder to keep his feelings out of it. Personal agendas had no place in a criminal investigation.

"Brody? What now?"

Brody sucked in renewed determination with a long breath. "What now? What now is nothing's changed. What'd you find on Vic's car?"

"Not much. Impound was anxious to take it away. I'm going down there first thing in the morning."

Brody scowled. "You do that. There's got to be paint from the other vehicle on it somewhere. I want that paint ID'd."

"And you? What are you going to do?"

"I'm going to carry on as if nothing's changed." Brody cleared his throat. "Nothing *has* changed."

Egan shook his head and turned on his heel. "I'm going to bed."

BRODY WOKE UP IN A cold sweat. He'd dreamed that Victoria was teetering on the edge of a cliff as a dark shadow slithered around her. She was screaming his name, but he couldn't get to her. The shadow was blocking him. Then it curled around her and she fell.

He sat up and wiped his face. Damn, he almost never remembered his dreams. But this one involved Victoria. Pushing himself up off the couch, he snagged his cell phone on the way out of his sitting room. He pounded on Egan's door, but the empty cup on the counter and the hollow sound of his knuckles on the metal door told him the Ranger sergeant was already gone.

Brody speed-dialed Hayes with his left hand as he reached into the fridge and grabbed an orange juice with his right. He downed the juice, and still Hayes's phone rang.

Growling in frustration, he slammed open the door to his sitting room just in time to see his bedroom door open.

Victoria came out, dressed in black pants, white top and a black-and-white-print sweater. Since it was summer and the temperature outside was well over ninety, he figured the sweater was to hide the bruises on her shoulder.

When she looked at him, her expression was carefully

neutral, but bright spots in her cheeks told him she wasn't as comfortable with what had happened the night before as she was pretending to be.

He blinked, trying to rid his brain of the image of her falling wrapped in shadow. "I thought you didn't have but one pair of black pants," he said.

"I picked up a few things when I was at the condos talking to Amanda Winger. Tammy Sutton called and invited me out for brunch." She lifted her chin a fraction.

"Is Kenneth Sutton going, too?"

"Yes. Do I have permission?"

Tammy and Kenneth Sutton. He'd already sized them up as single-mindedly ambitious, both of them. But were they murderers? He thought about Kimmie's phone call on the night she was killed. The call that could have saved her life, if he'd answered it.

Her voice on his voice mail had been choked with tears. *Brody? Why aren't you answering your cell phone? Call me. I'm at Taylor Landis's party. I need to talk to you. Mr. Sutton is probably going to fire me. I'm afraid he's really mad. Call me.*

He wished like hell he could refuse to let Victoria go, but she was probably almost as safe with the chairman of the city board and his wife as with Brody. Even if Sutton were behind the murders, he wouldn't dare risk his position by allowing something to happen to Victoria while she was out in public with him.

"I didn't realize you were such good friends with them."

"I'm not, but Tammy has been nice since all this happened. She's called me several times to do something with her, and I've turned her down every time. I'd prefer not to turn her down again. She offered to pick me up."

"Don't talk about what happened."

Her green eyes snapped to his, and he knew what she was thinking.

"About the hit-and-run," he said.

"Are you kidding? Kenneth and Tammy probably knew about it yesterday evening."

"How?"

Victoria gave a little laugh and shook her head. "The mayor…the police chief…who knows? But nothing, and I mean *nothing,* goes on around here that Tammy doesn't know about."

"Tell them you have to be back here by two, because this afternoon I want to drive the Anderson Loop with you. I want you to talk me through everything that happened."

"Yes, *sir.*" She walked across the sitting room to the door.

He couldn't blame her for her aloof, sarcastic response. He deserved it. In a way her attitude was a relief. She obviously regretted their…aberration as much as he did.

Still, she was pale and he could tell by the way she was moving that she was sore from her bruises.

"Vic, are you okay?"

She shot him an ironic glance. "Sure. I'm fine."

"If anything happens, *anything,* call me right away."

"With Tammy and Kenneth?" She laughed.

He caught her arm. "Kenneth Sutton said something to my sister on the night she was killed, something that upset her. Don't underestimate him."

"I knew she was upset. Everyone was talking about it. Are you saying Kenneth had something to do with the hit-and-run? He and Tammy were still at the party."

"I'm not dismissing *anybody,* not even if they have an ironclad alibi."

"I'll be careful."

"Keep your eyes and ears open, too." He let go of her arm before she could pull away.

BRODY SPENT THE MORNING reinterviewing the employees who worked both at Cantara Gardens and at the country club. The club manager, Michael DeCalley, arranged for the employees to come to the conference suite one at a time. There were seven workers who divided their time between the condos and the country club. Most of them were less than helpful. Either they knew nothing or they were excellent actors. But one young Hispanic woman, obviously several months pregnant, was visibly nervous.

"Your name is Eleana?"

She nodded, rubbing her tummy. "Yes. Eleana Mondavi. I work in the kitchen. I make the desserts."

"What about the condos? What do you do over there?"

"I don't work at the condos."

Brody assessed her. She was frightened of something. He made himself relax in his chair. If he was stiff and uptight, she'd be less likely to open up to him. "Mr. DeCalley sent you to talk to me because you have duties both at the condos and here."

Eleana looked down at her tummy and rubbed it more vigorously. "The baby kicks a lot," she said apologetically.

"When is your baby due?"

"In November." She smiled at him. "Not long, and yet very long."

Brody nodded. "Why did Mr. DeCalley send you here to talk to me?"

"Oh. I deliver the correspondence between here and the condos. It's only in the afternoon, before I leave work. I usually take it on my way home."

"What time is that?"

"I leave here before six o'clock."

"And where do you take the correspondence?" Brody asked.

"I place it in a box next to the manager's—Mr. Patterson's—apartment door." Eleana ducked her head and clasped her hands.

"And that's the only place you go inside the condos?"

"Yes, sir."

"Have you ever let anybody in? Or let anybody use your card or key?"

"No, sir."

Her answer was too quick, and she looked away.

"Eleana, are you sure?"

She glanced up at him. "Well…"

Brody clenched his jaw, forcing himself to remain relaxed. "Yes?"

"A week ago, on Wednesday, Mr. Woodward, the tennis man, followed me in. I told him I couldn't let him in, that he should call Mr. Patterson, but he just pushed against me and walked in when I did. He said he was visiting his friend."

Wednesday, the night Victoria was attacked.

"Friend? Who did he say his friend was?"

"Miles, I think. I don't remember his last name."

Miles Landis. Taylor Landis's freeloading brother. Brody shuddered at the idea of Carlson and Miles putting their heads together. He made a note on the pad in front of him.

"Has Carlson Woodward done that before? Or has anyone else?"

Eleana's face closed down. She wasn't going to tell him more. She shook her head. "No. No one else. Please, sir, I must go."

Brody stood and held out a hand to help Eleana rise. "Thanks, Eleana. You've been very helpful."

He talked with a couple of others, but Eleana's revelation was the most information he got.

As soon as he was done with the employees, he called Detective Sergeant Deason. "Pull in Miles Landis and Carlson Woodward. I have a witness who puts Woodward in the condos on Wednesday, the evening Victoria was attacked. According to what he told her, he was there to visit Landis. See what you can scare out of them."

"Will do. Woodward doesn't have access to the condos, does he?"

"Not according to the manager. And there's no card in his name. I'd like to find out how often he's there and how he gets in. This time he followed an employee in."

Just as Brody hung up from talking to Deason, his cell phone rang. It was Hayes.

"Where the hell have you been?" he said without preamble as soon as he picked up the phone. "I need you back here right—"

"Brody!" Hayes's voice was sharp with excitement. "I found the humidor. I'm leaving the pawnshop now."

"Great! Good going, Hayes. Are you sure it's Byron Dalloway's?"

"Dalloway mentioned a nick in the back left corner. It's the same one."

Brody closed his eyes as relief washed over him like a cool shower. Maybe this was the break he needed. "I don't suppose the owner could tell you who brought it in?"

"The owner wasn't there. I talked to a kid. He didn't know diddly except that he wanted two hundred dollars for the dang thing. The owner's supposed to open up the shop tomorrow morning. I'm going back to talk to him."

"Okay. What kind of shape is it in? Please tell me it hasn't been polished."

"I don't know, it looks pretty shiny, but I bagged it and I'm on the way to the lab this afternoon. We'll get the lab guys on it first thing in the morning."

"I want to hear as soon as you talk to the shop owner. We need everything he's got on whoever brought it in. Are there surveillance tapes?"

"I've got 'em. What'd you need me back there for? Isn't Egan there?"

"Yeah. He's processing Vic's car."

"Her car? What for?"

Brody quickly filled Hayes in on Victoria's brush with death.

"Damn. What the hell's going on there?"

"I don't know, but I'm going to find out. Stay there until you have something from the lab. I want prints, and I want them to match the partials we got off Vic's neck. I'm ready to stop this guy, whoever he is."

"Me, too, Brody. Me, too."

Brody heard Hayes take a long breath. "Brody? Can I talk to you about something?"

"Is it urgent?"

"No."

"Then let it wait. That humidor is priority. Got it?"

For a second, Hayes didn't say anything. "Got it," he said finally.

Brody hung up. He rubbed his eyes, thinking about Kimmie's death and the two men who had died since. He looked at the whiteboard, scanning the list of people who had used their access cards on the night of Victoria's attack.

He walked over and picked up the marker and wrote Carlson Woodward underneath Victoria's list. Then he wrote Eleana Mondavi.

How many times had Carlson bullied his way into the condos—or charmed his way in? He remembered Vic talking about him and his private lessons.

Brody's gut clenched in disgust. He'd always considered Carlson the worst kind of slimeball. There was nothing he wouldn't put past the man. Not even murder.

The hall door opened and Victoria walked in.

"Have fun?" Brody growled. He hadn't intended to growl—it just came out that way because of his dark thoughts.

"Not really."

"I guess brunch turned into lunch and cocktail hour."

"Well, it wasn't a total waste of time. I did enjoy eavesdropping on Kenneth Sutton."

Brody sent her a glance. Her eyes sparkled and her cheeks glowed, and his double-crossing body leaped into action. He clenched his jaw and turned back to the board. "Yeah?"

"After lunch, while we were finishing our coffee, Link Hathaway came up."

Hathaway. "That must have been a powerhouse meeting." Between them, Hathaway and Sutton controlled much of the business in San Antonio.

"Tammy kept talking, but luckily I was facing Kenneth, so I took a page from your playbook."

"My playbook?"

She nodded. "I looked bored and impatient, nodded at Tammy, and did my best to read their lips."

"Well?"

"Link said something about bids, and Kenneth nearly bit his head off."

"Bids?" Brody's brain zeroed in on the voice mail he'd received from Kimberly the night of the party. Sutton had been upset with her about something. Could it have been bids? Kimmie had mentioned irregularities with bids before.

"I didn't hear much, but my guess is that they were talking about the sealed bids put in by contractors for the new city library."

"Just how important are these bids?"

Victoria shrugged. "Every large project the city takes on has to be opened for bids from private contractors. The city planning board handles them. For a project like the library, for instance, the revenue could be in the tens of millions."

"So if somebody tampered with the bids, that would be a big deal."

"We're talking fraud involving local and federal funds. So yes, a very big deal. Anyone caught tampering with sealed bids would be staring at years in prison."

"People have murdered for less."

Victoria met his gaze. "You're saying that Kenneth or Link could be behind Gary's and Trent's murders? And Kimberly's?"

"Sutton and Kimmie had an argument the night of Taylor Landis's party. She called me, really upset." He dropped his gaze and turned back to the whiteboard.

Victoria watched his back and shoulders curl inward. *Pain.* He looked as if he'd been punched in the stomach. She wanted to reach out, to touch his shoulder and offer him comfort, but she didn't dare. Brody didn't invite comfort. When he hurt, he bore it alone.

She tried to keep the conversation as businesslike as possible. "I know. I remember that from the questioning that night, and from Gary's trial. When you talked to Kimberly, did she mention bids?"

He shook his head. "I didn't talk to…"

He swiped a hand down his face and then stalked over to the refrigerator and grabbed a bottle of water.

Victoria watched his throat move as he downed the water. When the bottle was nearly empty, he poured the last of it into his hand and splashed it on his face.

Her heart twisted in sympathy. He couldn't talk about his sister. His grief was still too new, too raw, even after eight months. She understood. It had taken her months to get over the razor-sharp pain that cut through her heart when her fiancé died. And she'd had her granddad to talk to. He'd taught her a lot about dealing with grief and heartache.

It was a cinch Brody hadn't talked to anybody. She went to his side and placed a hand on his back. "Brody, if you want to talk, I'll listen."

He turned his head and looked at her. His black, stabbing eyes cut her in two. But what almost knocked her to her knees was the dampness—she knew it wasn't water. Brody McQuade had tears in his eyes.

It was a good start.

Victoria rubbed his back and didn't say anything else. He'd talk when he was ready. Meanwhile, she could be there for him.

He straightened and stepped away. His demeanor transformed. The sadness and vulnerability were gone and he was one hundred percent Texas Ranger. He stalked back over to the whiteboard.

"Kimmie told me weeks before that something was going on with bids. She didn't say what. But the night of the Christmas party, Sutton apparently got very upset with her." His voice was as cold as his eyes.

Victoria sat down at the conference table. She didn't know what to say.

"Did you see the argument?" he asked her. "See them talking? Anything?"

She shook her head. "I told the police—and you—everything I saw. I didn't know Kimberly that well. We'd spoken a few times. All I know is that Caroline and Kimberly left suddenly, everyone was whispering, and Trent came up to me and said it was probably time to leave."

"So you left *after* Caroline Stallings and Kimmie? But you got to the intersection before them."

"Right. I had to maneuver around Caroline's Vette to get out of Tyler's driveway. She and Kimberly were sitting in it, talking. By the time I got my car clear so we could leave, Trent came out. He'd been trying to talk Gary into going with us."

"Zelke." Disdain dripped from Brody's lips.

Victoria knew he blamed Zelke for Kimberly's death, and her for defending him. But the paint chips her forensic analyst had found proved that another car had hit the Vette before Zelke's did.

"Can you remember who was still at the party when you left?"

Victoria frowned. "You know, all this is in the police reports."

Brody nodded impatiently. "I know. But there's a whole lot of difference in reading it in a typed report and talking to an eyewitness. I'd like to hear your description of the evening."

That she understood. It was the same reason she liked to have two adversaries in her office at the same time. People often said more than they meant to. And everybody noticed more than they realized. Once someone felt comfortable enough to talk easily, it was possible to find out all sorts of things.

"There were so many people there," she said. "It was hot and muggy, so people were drifting in and out. I know Kenneth and Tammy were still there by the time we left. And Link Hathaway. Obviously Taylor, since it was her house, and her brother Miles, who managed to hang around the buffet table all night."

"You're sure about Sutton?"

"Yes, I am. When Trent told me that he'd yelled at one of his interns, I succumbed to curiosity and looked around. He was talking on the phone. Oh…"

Brody shot her a glance. "What?"

"Like I said, Kenneth was standing in a reading alcove, talking on the phone. He looked up so I turned away. That's when I saw Tammy. She was on the other side of the room, and she was talking on her cell phone, too. I remember wondering if they were talking to each other."

"Could they have been?"

Victoria shrugged. "I suppose so. But get this. Trent almost ran into Link Hathaway on his way to get me to leave. Link was also on his cell phone. Something had definitely happened."

Brody's black eyes snapped. "Or was about to."

Chapter Eleven

It was after eight by the time Victoria and Brody got back from driving the Anderson Loop. Brody had insisted that she recount every minute of her harrowing experience.

The sight of the peeled-back guardrail and scarred pavement rekindled the terror of teetering on the edge of the world, trapped inside a hot metal car that at any second could become a coffin.

She'd wanted to see her car, but Brody had refused. It was being processed, he'd said. It would serve no purpose for her to see it.

He'd made her stand at the edge of the guardrail while she described everything she remembered about the car that had forced her off the road. He'd grilled her with an aggressiveness that more befitted a crack trial lawyer. At least he'd held on to her and kept her from getting too close to the edge.

By the time he was done with her, Victoria was amazed at how much her subconscious mind recalled, even during the terrifying moments when she'd thought she was going to plunge to her death.

Brody had latched on to her memory of the one vehicle that had roared past her on the winding road. A red Ferrari. Now as he unlocked the door to the conference suite and stood back to let her precede him inside, he talked to Egan on the phone.

"So how many have you talked to?"

Victoria took off her shoes and gestured toward the bedroom, indicating she was going to take a shower.

Brody didn't even acknowledge her. "I know," he said into the phone. "Nineteen. How hard can it be to locate nineteen people in this city who own red Ferraris?"

She went into the bedroom and closed the door, then plopped down on the bed with a sigh. The day had been oppressively hot, one of those scorching days when even the sun going down hadn't helped. And Brody had stopped the car at least a hundred times—well, ten, anyhow—and forced her to walk with him up and down the searing pavement, looking for any small sign, a skid mark, a scrape, that might yield a clue to the vehicle that had run her off the road.

She'd pointed out the obvious—that the SAPD crime-scene unit had combed the area—but in typical Brody fashion, he double-checked every inch himself. And it paid off. He'd found a tiny fleck of blue paint wedged between two bits of concrete paving. He'd knelt down and fished out the minuscule chip with his pocket knife and put it into an evidence bag.

Victoria had watched in fascination as he'd straightened and stood, his long thigh muscles straining the material of his tan dress pants. A wave of heat that had nothing to do with the weather washed through her. She took a deep breath and groaned quietly.

She'd known a lot of powerful men in her position as a partner in one of the most prestigious law firms in the city. Men whose strength took many forms, not just physical, but monetary, influence, control. But none of them compared to Brody McQuade. His power was physical, yes, but it was also built of integrity and leadership. When he was in the room, there was no doubt who was in charge.

She'd have loved to see him deal with the Cantara Hills Homeowners' Association. Men like Kenneth Sutton and Link Hathaway would have chafed at Brody telling them how to run their association.

Through the closed door, she heard Brody raise his voice, although she couldn't make out what he was saying. She knew he was talking to his sergeant, Egan Caldwell. The couple of times she'd met Egan, she'd gotten the impression he had a will of iron, too. It would be interesting to see those two butt heads.

She rubbed her eyes and forced herself to sit up. She had to have a shower. Right now she was so hot and tired her brain kept drifting. If she wasn't careful, within moments she'd be asleep.

Maybe a shower would help her shake off her torpor, and she could process everything she'd recalled today more rationally, without the heavy weight of fear squeezing her chest.

She opened the shower door, but after a second's hesitation, she filled the spa tub and relaxed in the swirling warm water for half an hour. Then she washed her hair under the jets and reluctantly climbed out. Her limbs felt steadier, and she felt clean and refreshed.

Now she was hungry.

She wrapped her kimono around her damp body and opened the bathroom door, anxious to dress and raid the little refrigerator in the conference room.

She ran smack into Brody's nearly naked body. "Oh!"

"Sorry."

Victoria clutched her kimono closed with both hands. "What are you...?"

The only thing covering him was a towel knotted at his lean

waist. His shoulders, arms and chest were slick with water, and droplets rained from his hair onto his forehead and neck.

"I needed some…boxers." Brody's words sounded apologetic, but he didn't seem to be able to take his eyes off the neckline of her kimono. "I thought I could get in and out before you finished in there."

Victoria swallowed. "I'll go back in." She gestured vaguely toward the bathroom. "I forgot…um…"

"Vic…"

She closed her eyes and felt herself surrendering to the low, sexy way his voice wrapped around the nickname he'd given her. Her insides quivered, her breasts tightened. How could a single syllable promise erotic delights beyond her wildest dreams?

His hot breath fanned her temple. His energy radiated toward her like body heat. She lifted her head slightly, longing for more than his breath to touch her.

But the brush of air turned cool. When she opened her eyes, he had his back to her and was reaching for the dresser drawers. "I'll get the rest of my clothes. I didn't mean to walk in on you."

"Brody—"

"When you're dressed, come on out. I'll order room service. Cold lobster salad for you, right? Should I order champagne?"

She heard the censure in his words. He would never let himself forget her status as a trust-fund baby.

"I'll make do with the white zinfandel, thanks," she said coolly.

Whirling, she stomped into the bathroom and slammed the door. She sat on the edge of the tub until she heard the bedroom door close.

BRODY PACED THE FLOOR. He wasn't good at waiting. Never had been. The day had started out badly. It was miserably hot, and Victoria obviously hadn't wanted to relive the most har-rowing experience of her life, hanging by a thread on the side of a limestone cliff.

Brody had forced her to relive every agonizing, terror-filled second. He'd hardened his heart and treated her like any other witness in a murder investigation.

She'd taken it, too, without a complaint. But the later it had gotten, the more pinched her expression had become, until by the time they got back here, she was pale as a ghost and about to collapse from the heat and the stress.

So in his stubborn way, after putting her through hell, he'd reacted defensively when she'd caught him in his bedroom—the room he'd given her, the room where he'd promised her she'd be safe. And to top it all off, he'd made a rude dig with that remark about the lobster salad and the champagne.

He was so frustrated in so many ways. He'd expected to hear back from Egan by now with the name of the owner of the red Ferrari, it had been over an hour since he'd ordered room service, and it was beginning to look like Victoria might not feel like socializing this evening.

A knock sounded on the door and at the same time, Brody's cell phone rang. He waved the room-service guy in and signed the ticket.

"Egan? What have you got?"

"We're in luck. I found the guy. Sometimes your bulldog-gish ways pay off. He's on his way out of town for two weeks. If we hadn't caught up to him today—"

"What'd he say? Did he remember the car?"

"Yeah. I've got his statement. He said it was an older-model Chevrolet. Said it looked like it had new paint."

"Could he ID the driver? Did he get a partial plate?"

"Listen to this, Brody. He thinks the plates started with

666. Obviously, he remembered that. And he thinks it might have been a Lumina or a Caprice. But that was all he saw."

"Have you talked to Deason?"

"Nope. Not yet."

"Call him now. Get him the Ferrari guy's statement and let the police track down that vehicle. I need you back in Austin."

"Again?"

"Right. You and Hayes are working in the lab tomorrow. Hayes found the humidor."

"No way! That's great! Fingerprints?"

"That's what he's going to be doing tomorrow. I want you there, Caldwell. I need one hundred percent infallibility on the chain of evidence. With you and Keller, I can be assured that nobody can question our findings."

"What about tracking down this Chevy?"

"The cops can handle that. As soon as they locate the vehicle, I want a paint sample compared to the sample I picked up at the scene and the fleck we retrieved from Caroline Stallings's car."

"I'll get with Deason and then I'll head on up to Austin. Maybe we'll catch a break."

Brody massaged his neck. "I sure as hell hope so. Nobody will be happier than me to get this case over and done with. I've about had it with Cantara Hills."

VICTORIA EASED THE BEDROOM door closed. Her ears burned with irritation and, if she was truthful, humiliation. Her grandmother had always told her that eavesdroppers never heard anything good about themselves, and she'd just proved it.

She'd pouted for a few minutes after Brody's champagne remark, but the idea of lobster salad and a glass of wine had lured her out. Of course she would have been equally happy with a taco and iced tea, but Brody hadn't given her the chance to tell him.

Just as she'd eased the bedroom door open, she'd heard Brody talking to one of his fellow Rangers. He'd sounded tired but upbeat, as if something had broken in the case. Her heart had leaped—maybe finally there was some good news, but then he'd thrown out that comment about Cantara Hills.

She shouldn't have taken it personally, but how could she not? He was talking about where she lived—her neighbors, her home…*her.* In a way she understood. Sometimes she felt like she'd had it with the snobbery and the posturing and the whole sense of entitlement that permeated this exclusive area of San Antonio.

And to be fair, Brody had made it clear from the beginning how he felt about her and her *trust-fund*-baby neighbors.

Still—maybe she was overly sensitive—his words hurt.

A brisk knock sounded on the door, and Victoria realized she was sitting on the edge of the bed with her arms wrapped around herself.

"Victoria, dinner's here."

His voice through the door grated on her nerves. It was so…neutral, so just-the-facts-ma'am. He didn't even call her Vic. How had he ever turned her on with just the sound of his voice?

"I'm not hungry," she yelled back. "I'm going to bed."

"You've got to eat," he said evenly, spouting that maddeningly even tone that drove her nuts. "Besides, I need to talk to you."

"About what? Some break in the case that will get you out of Cantara Hills that much faster? Congratulations."

He knocked again. "Victoria, come out here or I'll come in and get you."

She looked down at herself. She'd put on red-silk lounging

pajamas with long, flowing sleeves. How ridiculous! What had she been thinking? She jumped up and ran over to the closet where the floor was littered with her dirty clothes. She rooted around until she found the baggy T-shirt and madras shorts. Both were wrinkled, and the T-shirt had a small stain of pizza sauce on the front, but she didn't care. She threw them on and twisted her damp hair up into a messy ponytail. She stomped over and threw the door open.

"I heard your cell..." she started, but there was nobody there. She stomped across the sitting room and opened the door to the conference room, but all the stomping and slamming lost much of its punch when she had to do it twice.

Brody was sitting at the conference table, shoveling lobster salad into his mouth and washing it down with beer. He barely looked up. "Your salad's wilting."

"I heard your cell ring—any news?" She folded her arms and glared at him. But he kept on eating, and try as she might, she couldn't keep her gaze from drifting to the beautifully pre-sented salad with the big pink chunks of lobster artfully arranged on top. French-toast rounds garnished the plate, and next to the salad was a tiny lemon tart with raspberry syrup drizzled over it. Her stomach growled loudly.

Brody's mouth quirked up.

"Well, it's a shame to let it go to waste," she muttered. She stalked over to the table and sat. As she dug in, Brody finished. He sat back and up-ended his beer.

"So?" she said around a mouthful of lobster.

"Hayes found the humidor."

"Byron's humidor? Where?"

"In a pawnshop just outside of Austin. He's taking it to the lab to lift fingerprints. We're hoping one of the prints will match the partial I got off your neck."

Victoria's hand flew to her neck. She shuddered. "Oh, I'd almost forgotten about that." She still saw the bruises when she looked in the mirror, but they had faded to a pale, ugly green that didn't compare with the discoloration that ran from her shoulder to her hip.

Brody sat up and peered at her neck. He ran his thumb along the still-tender skin. "They're almost gone," he said.

She did her best to ignore the erotic sensation of his warm fingers brushing her skin. "So you were right about the things that were taken from the apartments? The killer had no use for them? He got rid of them for money?"

"Looks that way. The guy at the pawnshop where Hayes found the humidor didn't remember a diamond-and-emerald bracelet. Maybe our perp pawned it somewhere else, or maybe he kept it for his girlfriend."

Victoria finished the lobster and was picking at bits of lettuce and celery. "What about the print from my neck? No matches?"

Brody shook his head. "In the first place, you're an attorney. You know it's never a sure thing to match a print."

"I'm a corporate lawyer. I've never tried a criminal case. The closest I ever came was representing Gary in the hit-and-run."

Brody frowned.

"Anyway, they always seem to match them on television."

"Trust me, it's not that easy."

Brody picked up the room-service tray and reached for her plate. She put a hand over his.

"Wait. Leave me the lemon tart."

He shook his head and left both tarts on the table, then quickly cleared away the dishes and set them on the floor near the door.

"It all depends," he said, "on whether the perp has a record or has been printed for some other reason. Then the partial has to have enough clarity to match. Sometimes the print is too smudged or faint to get a computer match. Yours, for instance, was right on the edge of unreadable. In that case, it has to be matched by a human eye, and that's definitely a long shot. And hard to prove in court."

"The print on my neck was too faint?"

"We were lucky to get anything at all."

The memory of her attacker's hands on her neck, his weight on top of her, sent chills down Victoria's spine.

She wrapped her hand around the cold glass and sipped at her champagne. "What are we doing tomorrow?"

He straightened. "You're not doing anything. I'm meeting with Detective Sergeant Deason about the evidence they've gathered, and then I've got another meeting with the homeowners' association to coordinate the installation of the new security system. There'll be a couple of hours when the condos won't have security. I plan to be there, along with several officers and some private security guards hired by the homeowners' association. And depending on what Egan and Hayes find, I may need to go to Austin."

"Isn't there anything I can do?"

"You can stay here—safe—so I don't have to worry about you."

"I could go with you. As long as I'm with you, we both know I'm safe."

Brody's dark gaze met hers and for an instant she felt as if she were swimming in a pool of bittersweet chocolate. The thing between them rose to life. Sometimes it roared like a dragon, but other times, like now, it felt like a spider's silk, winding around her, pulling her toward him. No matter whether she wanted to be or not, she was bound to him by silvery, invisible threads.

"Brody?" She had no idea why she said his name. No idea what she was asking for. Not just sex, although that was a part of it. She craved him, now that she'd had him. His hot, powerful body wrapped around hers, his pulsing heat inside her in that most intimate joining, his whole attention focused on her. That was safety.

He stepped closer. His palms slid up her arms, warm and possessive. He bent his head and she closed her eyes, but the deep erotic kiss didn't come.

Instead, he kissed her temple, a heartbreakingly sweet kiss, but not a lover's.

Her eyes flew open.

"Get some sleep, Vic. Your job is to stay safe. I've got an employee of a private security agency to guard you tomorrow." He dug in the pocket of his jeans. "Here's a photo of him. His name is Lou Riviera. Do not open the door to anyone else. If he doesn't show up, call me immediately, or call Detective Sergeant Deason. You have the gun I gave you."

Victoria nodded, swallowing nervously.

"When do you use the gun?" he asked.

"Only if someone threatens my life."

"Remember, Vic, if you pull that trigger, you can never take it back. Riviera will be armed. Maybe it would be better if you didn't carry the gun, because if you freeze up, your attacker can take it from you and use it on you."

Victoria lifted her chin. "If you're not with me, I want to be armed. That man was on top of me, choking me. I couldn't do anything to stop him. I don't ever want to be that helpless again."

"I swear, Vic, I'll get him if it's the last thing I do."

Chapter Twelve

By the time Victoria got up the next morning, Brody was gone. A brief inspection told her the suites were empty. She opened the curtains in the sitting room, which looked out over the pool. A good-looking Hispanic guy stood near the pool. She recognized him from the photo Brody had given her.

His biceps strained the material of a white short-sleeved shirt that sported a badgelike logo on the breast pocket. The black leather holster belted around his waist and his toned body made him look very official and very competent.

He smiled and mouthed, "Good morning." Then he took a step backward and planted his feet and clasped his hands behind him in the classic military at-ease posture.

She was impressed. He understood body language. He appeared capable, even formidable, and at the same time unthreatening toward her. Leave it to Brody to find the best bodyguard in San Antonio.

She unlocked the doors.

"Ms. Kirkland, I'm Lou Riviera. I work for San Antonio Security Systems. I'll be here all day, guarding you, while Lieutenant McQuade is out. Is there anything I can do for you?"

"Good morning, Mr. Riviera. Bro—the lieutenant told me about you."

"Call me Lou."

"Thank you. You can call me Victoria. I can't think of a thing you can do for me except keep the bad guys away." She smiled and he smiled back. He really was a nice-looking guy.

"I was just about to order breakfast," she said. "May I order you something?"

Riviera shook his head. "I ate earlier, but it looks like it's going to be a scorcher today. Orange juice and water would be great."

"We've got all the water you could need in here. There's a small refrigerator in the main conference room. I'll order a tall glass of orange juice with breakfast. Do you think it would be all right if I sat out by the pool to eat?"

Riviera grinned, showing even, white teeth. "I think you can do whatever you want, as long as I'm right beside you."

As she closed the doors and picked up the phone to order breakfast, she felt a shiver of fear along her spine. Lou Riviera was charming and handsome and completely at ease around her, but the fact remained that he was there because someone wanted her dead.

BRODY MADE IT THROUGH the changeover of the security system at the Cantara Gardens Condominiums without a hitch. Once again, he saw proof of the old adage that wealth had its privileges.

Apparently a phone call from Kenneth Sutton was all it took to get a custom-designed security system ready and delivered in four days. The company's tech guys were at the condos by seven o'clock in the morning and finished by just after nine. Brody had seized the opportunity to talk with Sutton again.

He'd questioned the businessman back in December about the argument he'd had with Kimberly on the night of her death. At the time, Sutton had sidestepped the question by claiming it was a work disagreement. He'd had a couple of drinks and was short-tempered.

He'd apologized sincerely for upsetting Kimmie. Although Brody pegged Sutton as a prime suspect, he had to admit that no one could have faked the clammy pallor and the shock on Sutton's face that night.

Today, with eight months' healing time since the death of his sister, and without much more proof than he'd had back then, Brody still didn't have a better suspect than Sutton. And he wanted him to know it.

"Phone call?" Sutton repeated the gist of Brody's question. "I don't remember making a phone call." He looked genuinely bewildered. "Hell, it was probably Tammy calling me from across the room to tell me she was ready to leave." Sutton chuckled. "She does that all the time."

"I'm sure when we check your phone records and your wife's, they'll back that up."

Sutton's brows drew down. "I'm sure they will. What's going on here? I know you're dead set on proving that the murders in Cantara Gardens are connected with your sister's death. But you can't think I had anything to do with it."

"Kimmie called me on the night she was killed. She was upset about something you'd said to her. What was that about? Something about missing sealed bids, maybe?"

"Look, McQuade, I went over all that with the police at the time. We had some irregularities involving bids, but it had nothing to do with Kimberly or me. She was a great kid. Everybody loved her."

Sutton shook his head impatiently. "But face it, she was a

kid. I don't remember what upset her so much that night, but I can tell you, every intern I've ever had has been moon-struck over the amount of money the city planning board deals with. And the sealed-bid process is complicated."

Sutton stopped walking and turned to Brody. "Like I said, I'd had a couple of drinks, and I wasn't interested in talking business. I might have said something mean, and I regret that I upset her, but I never threatened to fire her."

Brody stepped out through the front doors of the condos with Sutton right behind him. He didn't contradict Sutton, but he had Kimmie's message on his phone, if it came to that.

"I can guarantee you one thing, Sutton," he said. "Kimmie wasn't moonstruck about money. Power maybe, but not money."

Sutton turned to him and held out his hand. Brody was oddly reluctant to accept the hand the smooth businessman offered. Or maybe not so oddly, considering that it was Sutton who'd upset Kimmie and precipitated the events that led to her death. He hesitated, but finally took Sutton's hand. "I'll be in touch about your phone records," Brody said. "I'm sure it will clear everything up."

"I want to thank you for kicking our butts about the security system," Sutton said. "I feel better already. Maybe the break-ins and attacks will stop now."

"I don't think so. Victoria's life has been threatened more than once."

Sutton sent Brody a thoughtful glance. "Are you sure what's happening to Victoria is connected to the break-ins? She dated a train wreck of a playboy, name of Rayburn Andrews, for a long time. If that's her taste in men, her problem may be with an ex."

Brody's knuckles itched to feel Sutton's capped teeth

crunch against them, but he kept his cool. "My evidence suggests otherwise," he said evenly, gratified when Sutton's eyes widened in sudden apprehension.

Sutton paused for a few seconds, but Brody held his tongue. He wasn't giving out any information to anybody. Especially his certainty that Sutton was in this up to his eyeballs.

"Well, here's my car," Sutton said unnecessarily. "I'd better get going." As he walked toward his car, Vincent Montoya got out and opened the back door. He was the consummate chauffeur. He didn't even glance at Brody.

Brody watched the car drive away before he got into his Jeep.

Had Sutton's phone call been to someone who'd lain in wait and hit Caroline Stallings's car on purpose? Montoya maybe? Was Kenneth Sutton guilty of murder, or just guilty of being a slimeball?

As Brody cranked his Jeep and prepared to leave, his cell phone rang. It was Deason.

"McQuade, we got a probable match on the license plate of the car that rammed Victoria."

"What? Who is it? Have you picked him up?"

"Whoa, hold your horses. Like I said, it's a *probable*, not an exact match. Its first three digits are 666. But there are several thousand plates with 666 as the first three letters. Frankly I'm surprised they even print plates with that number on them."

"So how are you narrowing it down?"

"Both Victoria and the driver of the Ferrari described it as an older, dark-blue Chevrolet sedan. That cuts the field down to ninety-seven vehicles."

"Ninety-seven." Brody sighed. Then he remembered the paint chip from Caroline Stallings's car. "Dark blue isn't the original color, remember? The paint chip Vic's forensic specialist analyzed had dark blue over dark green paint, plus two types of primer."

Deason snorted. "Way ahead of you there, Lieutenant. I've got three vehicles with that partial plate that are registered as dark green and are now dark blue."

Brody's heart leaped in his chest. "Three?"

"Right. One is a teenage boy who painted his car in his high-school shop class. The second is an older lady, and the third is a guy named Harold Young. Thing is, Young's been dead for two years. Someone's been sending in his registration."

Brody didn't want to get his hopes up, but they were already soaring. "This could be it!"

"I've got a couple of officers checking out Young's LKA. We'll see what turns up."

"If the guy's dead, his last-known address is probably meaningless by now."

"I'll let you know what I find out."

"Thanks, Deason."

So they'd identified the car. It wasn't much, but it was more than he'd been able to put together up until now. Essentially a bunch of names on a whiteboard and a bunch of incidents that only he seemed able to connect.

The most frustrating thing for Brody was that while he'd kept everybody busy running down leads and searching for clues, he felt like he'd done nothing except babysit Victoria— not that it was a chore.

It occurred to him that at some point his focus had changed. This was no longer just about avenging his sister's death and nabbing the SOB who'd killed her. Somewhere along the way he'd found another purpose, another life that meant as much to him as Kimmie's had. Victoria's.

As much as Kimmie's? He rubbed his temples. When had that happened? For as long as he could remember, his baby sister had been the one person he loved more than anything. His parents had been there—sort of, between their great adventures. But Kimmie had always been his family, his responsibility. When she'd died, he'd been sure his heart could never open up enough to love anyone that much again.

As if to mock him, Victoria's beautiful face rose in his mind and his chest squeezed with a sweet, painful ache.

Doing his best to ignore it, he checked his watch and saw nothing but bare wrist. *Damn.* He'd left it on the side table in his suite.

His gaze slid to the clock on the dashboard. At least he didn't have to worry about Victoria today. He'd hired Lou Riviera to guard her, which left him free to do some investigating on his own. He'd told Lou not to leave her side until he got back. He'd used Lou before. He was a topnotch bodyguard and investigator, employed by the most highly-thought-of security agency in the area. He could feel assured that she was safe.

He pushed the call-back button on his cell phone. "Deason, I want to go with the officers to check out Young."

"Sure. Tell you what. I'll meet you there." Deason gave him the address.

A visceral thrill ran through Brody's gut. He'd always loved fieldwork the most. Being a lieutenant had its good points. It satisfied his natural leadership instincts. But sitting behind a desk analyzing data and filling out reports could be boring as hell.

Today, though, he was a Ranger. And before the day was out, he would be at least one step closer to finding the man who'd killed his sister.

VICTORIA PRESSED THE channel-up button on the remote control for the seventy-seventh time. And each click had upped her irritation and escalated her boredom. She paused on a weather channel. The day was destined to be a real scorcher, as Lou had said. San Antonio was in the middle of a heat wave that wasn't going anywhere anytime soon.

She tossed the remote down and stepped over to the French doors. There was nobody sitting out by the pool. They were probably all either in the dining room drinking a cold drink or on the other side in the air-conditioned indoor pool.

Even Lou had knocked on the door about twenty minutes earlier and told her he'd move inside to the hall outside the conference suite for a while, if it was all right with her. She'd tried to get him to come inside and have a cold drink, but he'd declined.

"If Lieutenant McQuade found me sitting with my feet propped up and drinking a bottle of water like a card-carrying member of the country club," he'd said, "he'd have my job."

Victoria had protested, but Lou had stood firm. She thought Brody would like the idea of Lou being glued to her side, but she didn't want to get him in trouble.

She put her palm against the glass of one of the French doors. It was hot to the touch. Behind her the morning weather girl was ecstatic that temperatures were expected to exceed 103.

Bored and restless, Victoria let her gaze wander around Brody's sitting room. There wasn't much of *him* there, but that wasn't surprising. These were temporary quarters. He'd been here a week, and probably in less than another week he'd be gone.

He lived and worked in Austin. And while in reality the

state's capital was only a little over an hour away, it might as well be on the other side of the earth.

The thought saddened her, which was ridiculous. Brody McQuade meant nothing to her—or at least he shouldn't. He was a lawman with a job to do. When this job was done, he'd move on to the next job.

And once her life was no longer threatened, she'd go back to her ordinary life.

But whether it made sense or not, the idea of Brody no longer being in her life, no longer worrying about her, no longer close enough that she could breathe in his warm fresh scent, broke her heart.

Her gaze lit on the side table. He'd left his watch. It was sitting on top of a small stack of papers. She'd never paid any attention to his watch, except to note that he always wore it. She stepped over to the table and picked it up. *Heavy.*

As soon as she looked at it she knew what it was. It was a Tag Heuer Carrera. At least three grand retail. She was surprised.

In the first place, Brody didn't seem the kind of guy who cared about affecting an expensive, trendy watch. And in the second place, who knew Texas Rangers made that kind of money?

She slipped it onto her wrist, feeling like a little girl playing dress-up. The watch face more than spanned the width of her wrist. As she fingered the stainless-steel case, she felt something on its back.

Slipping the watch off, she turned it over. It was engraved. She switched on the lamp and held the back of the watch close to the light.

For my big bro Brody. HB, love, Kimmie. And then the date. *HB.* Happy birthday? So Brody was a Scorpio. It shouldn't have surprised Victoria. He certainly had the sting. But he also had an unexpectedly gentle side.

Victoria started to lay the watch back down where she'd found it when the oddity of the year hit her. The date was six years earlier. Kimberly would have been no more than nineteen. Where would a nineteen-year-old get that kind of money?

A scant memory tugged at the edge of her brain. A word that had flashed across her vision from one of the papers under the watch. She sent a slightly furtive glance toward the conference room—a reflex, because she knew she was alone. Then she let her gaze fall to the stack of papers.

There, sticking out from underneath a bill. It was a manila folder from an estate attorney, with the words "Kimberly Noelle McQuade Estate" scrawled across the front and a pink sticky note attached. The sticky note read, "B.McQ. Just sign where indicated and return. The estate will revert to you. Thanks."

Estate? Brody had an estate? The more she stared, the more her surprise morphed into anger. She felt like screaming in frustration, jumping up and down like a spoiled brat— a trust-fund spoiled brat.

The one thing she'd counted on with Brody was his integrity, his truthfulness. Okay, she'd counted on a lot more than that, but she'd believed in his innate honesty.

He'd lied to her. He'd been so contemptuous of her wealth. He'd called her a trust-fund baby, as if the name was a vile curse. He'd curled his lip at her dislike of beer. He'd made fun of her lobster salad.

Victoria was so angry her ears were burning. He was the worst kind of snob—a snob and a liar. A vague, sick feeling wrapped around her heart. She couldn't think of any reason he'd hide his wealth from her.

But then, she couldn't think of any reason he owed her an explanation, either.

Still, if he couldn't bother to be truthful with her, then why should she bother being such a good little victim?

He'd told her he was hiring a bodyguard to keep her safe, but he hadn't said anything about where they could or couldn't go. At least not overtly.

She stomped into the bedroom to dress. She didn't deserve to be punished for being a *victim*. Obviously there was no reason for her to have to stay there in that cramped, claustrophobic bedroom, except that Brody McQuade wanted it that way.

"Well, that's just tough, Lieutenant," she muttered, tossing her kimono on the bed. As long as she kept Lou with her, she could go anywhere she wanted and be just as safe as she would be here. And she had a couple of places she wanted to go.

BRODY MET DETECTIVE Sergeant Deason on St. Mary's Street. It was a run-down barrio on the south side of San Antonio. When he pulled to the curb behind the police car, his heart sank. The tiny rowhouses had a gap in them, like a missing tooth. Where Young had lived was a burned-out shell.

Deason was standing with a uniformed officer in front of the burned-out building, rubbing the top of his balding head as the officer talked and gestured.

Brody walked up in time to hear the officer say something about the neighbors.

"Anyone remember Young or the car?" he asked without preamble.

Deason wiped a trickle of sweat from his forehead and slung it away. "Officer Barnes, this is Lieutenant McQuade of the Rangers. I think you may have met him the night of the attack on Ms. Kirkland at Cantara Gardens."

"Yes sir." The officer nodded at Brody.

"Tell the lieutenant what you've found out."

Barnes pulled a small notepad from his shirt pocket and flipped a few pages. "The family living in the next house up just moved in a year ago, after the fire. The folks on the other side—the Guzmans—knew Young. Said he was a drunk, a loud one. Fell asleep with a cigarette one night." The officer flipped another page. "Mrs. Guzman said he would have killed them all if his daughter hadn't woken up."

"Daughter?" Brody turned from surveying the blackened mess that was once someone's home. "She didn't die in the fire, did she?"

"No, sir. She called the fire department. Too late for her dad, but she got out and alerted the neighbors." Barnes pointed at the Guzmans' house. "You can see some fire damage, but no one else was hurt."

Brody nodded and walked over to the burned-out building. He slid his hands into his pockets and kicked at a charred board with the toe of his boot. "Where's the daughter now?"

"Mrs. Guzman told me she'd seen her a few months ago. She was asking about the company that rents the houses."

"Maybe thinking about suing for wrongful death," Deason added.

He turned to Barnes. "Did you find out anything about her?"

"No, sir. But Mrs. Guzman is home."

Brody turned on his heel and headed for the Guzman house. As he stepped onto the minuscule porch stoop, the front door opened.

"Hola, Señora Guzman," he said, removing his hat. *"¿Cómo esta usted? Me llamo Lieutenant McQuade. Soy un Texas Ranger."*

"Good morning, Lieutenant. You are very charming, and your Spanish is passable, but I think my English is better." She stepped out onto the stoop, wiping her hands on a dish towel. "You have more questions about Harold?" She glanced toward the burned house.

"Yes, ma'am. Actually about his daughter. Did you know her?"

"Of course. She would come over here when he got drunk. She and my son were friends in school."

"Do you know where she is now?"

Mrs. Guzman shook her head. "Working for some rich people somewhere. When I saw her a few months ago, she was *embarazada.*" Mrs. Guzman clicked her tongue.

"Pregnant?" Brody's heart slammed against his chest. He gulped in air, telling himself it was a coincidence. Warning himself not to get his hopes up. "What's her name?"

"Eleana. Pretty girl. I didn't see no wedding ring."

"Eleana Young?" His pulse hammered in his ears.

"No, no. Harold was not her real father." Mrs. Guzman slung her towel over her shoulder and shook her head. "Her mother's name was Mondavi. Eleana Mondavi. Lieutenant, are you all right?"

Brody's mouth was so dry he could hardly swallow. *Eleana Mondavi.* "Yes, ma'am. Thank you."

"You see Eleana, you tell her my Carlos is in Iraq. You tell her she should have married him when he asked her."

Brody stalked back to Deason's side. "Young's stepdaughter works at the country club. Eleana Mondavi. She's in this up to her eyeballs. I want her picked up, *now!*"

BRODY HAD JUST PULLED onto the interstate when his cell phone rang. He pulled it out. It was Egan. "McQuade. What's up, Caldwell?"

"Brody!" Egan's voice was sharp with excitement. "I hope you're sitting down. We got hits on the prints."

Brody's fingers spasmed around the phone. He fought to keep his voice steady. This was the break he'd been afraid would never come. The identity of the person who'd killed his sister.

"Hits? Whose?"

"Three sets. Dalloway of course. And Carlson Woodard."

"Carlson? Damn. Are you sure?"

"Absolutely. His prints are on file from a couple of DUIs."

The heat of fury surged through Brody's veins. "That weasel. Could he have done this?"

"Brody, the third set match a Vincent Montoya. He's got a sheet for grand theft auto."

"Montoya? That's Sutton's chauffeur."

Egan was silent for a second. "So the chauffeur did it? That's rich."

Brody ignored Egan's bitter words. "What about the print from Victoria's neck? Any match?"

"The print from her neck is consistent with Montoya's right forefinger. Can't say it's a slam dunk, but the two prints have about a fifty-percent match."

"Caldwell, get back here right now. Call Deason to get a warrant to search everything Montoya ever even thought about owning—house, car, storage facilities, safe-deposit boxes, garbage cans. Don't leave out anything. Soon as you've got the warrant, pick him up. I'm on my way to question an employee of the country club. Her father is the owner of the car that hit Kimmie and ran Vic off the road."

"Got it. What about Carlson?"

"Get Hayes down here to help. Tell Deason to have Carlson picked up and interrogated within an inch of his disgusting life. I don't think he killed anybody, but nothing else would surprise me."

"I'm with you on that."

"Once you've got evidence from the search, Hayes can hand-carry it back to the lab. With any luck we'll have Montoya's prints to process, paint chips to compare, and who knows what else once we get our hands on that car. This is the break we've been waiting for."

His phone beeped. "I've got another call. I'll talk to you later."

"I'm on my way."

The other caller was Deason. Brody answered. "Caldwell just let me know we got a match on prints," he said.

"Lieutenant—"

Brody stopped. "Yeah?" He didn't like the tone of Deason's voice. "What is it?"

"Eleana Mondavi left work early."

"Early? How early?"

"About an hour ago."

"Mrs. Guzman must have called her. Have you checked her house? Called her cell phone?"

"Yes. We're taking every possible step to find her. I've talked to DeCalley at the country club, as well as Patterson at the condos, and I've dispatched two officers to her house, just in case there's been foul play."

"What about the hospitals? She's pregnant. Something could have happened with the baby."

"That, too. I've even got a BOLO out to airports, rental-car agencies and bus stations."

Brody wiped his face. A *be on the lookout for* was a great

tool for stopping fleeing criminals or even searching out victims in hiding. "Great. Thanks, Deason. I appreciate it." He took a deep breath. "Now listen. The prints we lifted off the humidor and off Vic's neck belong to Vincent Montoya. He's Kenneth Sutton's driver. He and Eleana must be connected. Sergeant Caldwell is probably calling you right now about getting a warrant to search everything Montoya ever touched."

"You want us to pick him up?"

"Let Caldwell go with you, if you don't mind. And as soon as you've got him in custody, let me know. I want to question that lowlife myself."

Chapter Thirteen

Brody headed to Kenneth Sutton's house, hoping to catch Montoya there. He could bring him in for questioning and hold him until Deason secured the warrant.

He got out of his jeep and strode to the front door. Before he had a chance to ring the bell, the door swung open. It was Tammy Sutton, in a slinky silk robe that looked kind of like Vic's kimono, except that while Vic looked exotic and sexy in hers, Tammy looked as if she'd been interrupted in the middle of sex. Her hair was mussed and the robe gaped open in front, revealing a little bralike thing underneath.

"Lieutenant…?"

"McQuade. Brody."

"Right, Brody." Tammy smiled and raised a perfect brow. "Is there something I can *do* for you this morning, Brody?"

Brody clamped his jaw and reminded himself why he was here. "Is your husband here?"

"Why no, he's at the office. Now why would you think he'd be here at this time of day?" Her smile turned catlike.

She was baiting him. If he made a move on her, he had a feeling she wouldn't turn him down. Not that he was even tempted, but he'd seen her type. She was definitely a cougar.

"Actually I wanted to talk with Vincent Montoya."

Tammy's soft gaze turned hard and curious. "Montoya? Whatever for?"

"Just some routine questions."

"I see. He drove Kenneth in to work this morning as usual."

Brody clenched his jaw. She wasn't going to make this easy. And in about ten seconds she was going to ask him to come in.

"What does Montoya do after he drives Sutton to work?"

Tammy chuckled and pressed a hand against her exposed cleavage. "Goodness, Lieutenant. You do have a lot of questions. Why don't you come in? I can offer you something."

He ignored her implication. "No. That won't be necessary. Montoya?"

"What does he do? Oh, I don't know. I think he's free until Kenneth needs him. Possibly for a lunch meeting, possibly not until he leaves for the day."

"He never comes back here?"

"Not usually. I drive myself."

Brody's cell phone rang. He pulled it out. It was Egan. Maybe they'd found something at Montoya's house. He touched the brim of his hat.

"Thank you, Mrs. Sutton. I appreciate your help."

"Anytime, Lieutenant. Come back when you can stay longer."

Brody answered his phone as he headed back to his car. "McQuade."

"Brody, we got our warrant and we're at Montoya's house. He's an interesting guy."

"Get to it, Caldwell."

"It looks to me like he's got what you might call a *used-car* business going."

"You mean a chop shop? So he's got car-painting equipment?"

"He's got a full-service body shop in a building behind his house."

"The warrant covers that, right?"

"You bet. We're collecting paint samples now. I've got a feeling we're going to find the same paint we took off Victoria's car—and from the Stallings woman's car."

"Well, hurry it up. Montoya apparently has his mornings free after he drives Sutton into work, so he may show up."

"Great. We'll be ready for him."

VICTORIA LOOKED AT HERSELF in the mirror. She looked cool and confident in a slim skirt and a crisp white blouse. On her feet were white, high-heeled, backless sandals, and on her face was a look of fierce determination.

She consciously relaxed her jaw. She knew it was going to take some persuading to convince Lou Riviera that he could guard her just as efficiently at the Cantara Gardens Condominiums as he could here.

She'd wanted Brody to question Jane Majorsky, the boutique owner whose emerald bracelet had been stolen, but as far as she knew, he hadn't. And the one time she'd had the chance, Jane hadn't answered her door.

She knew Jane had let Carlson Woodward use her access card at least once to get into the condos. She'd seen him coming in. Jane was one of his *private* tennis students. She felt sure that with a little shared gossip, she could find out a lot about Carlson.

She pasted a smile on her face. Then she patted her hair. "Okay, Victoria," she murmured. "If you can't charm a good-looking guy into taking you where you want to go, then you deserve to stay cooped up in this suffocating room."

She raised an eyebrow at her reflection. A niggle of doubt tickled the edge of her brain. Lou had refused to sit down because he'd thought Brody wouldn't approve. How much more would Brody object to Lou's allowing her out of the country club, even if he was right beside her?

She took a long breath. "You're just lucky it's not Brody out there."

She smoothed the front of her blouse, and her fingernail snagged the material. "Dammit." She ran the tip of a finger over the chipped nail of her ring finger.

She glanced at her watch as she searched in her makeup kit for a fingernail file.

Clutching the metal file and worrying the chipped nail with her thumb, she walked through the sitting room and out into the conference room.

She opened the hall door with a smile, only to find the hall empty. A frisson of fear slid down her spine. Where was Lou?

Come on, Victoria. He probably went to the bathroom, or walked back around to the pool side.

She closed the door and went back into the sitting room. The curtains were open and the sun was glaring on the glass of the French doors.

Victoria peered out at the pool. The place was empty, except for one lone kid out in the triple-digit heat. It was a teenage boy who looked like he'd already gotten too much sun. As she watched, he turned over onto his stomach and emptied the last of a bottle of water over his head.

Victoria paced the sitting room.

Should she call Brody? Should she go out and look for Lou? *No!*

She almost jumped. She'd have sworn that was Brody's voice barking at her.

Okay, okay. She'd be a good girl and wait. It was less than twenty minutes until Lou's regular hourly check-in.

Just as she started to file her chipped nail, a brisk knock sounded on the hall door.

Lou. Thank goodness. She hurried over to the door and grabbed the knob. But that feeling of fear was still tingling at the base of her spine. Where had he been?

"Lou?" she called out. It was silly, but better safe than sorry.

No answer.

"Lou?" she called a little louder. "Is that you?" She looked through the peephole in the door, and saw Lou's white shirt filling her vision.

Thank goodness. She unlocked the dead bolt.

The door slammed into her and knocked her backward. Burning shock paralyzed her.

"What—" she started.

"Shut up!"

It wasn't Lou. This man was shorter, bulkier. And he smelled like Torture cologne.

Shock gave way to panic. It was the man who'd strangled her. She stared at him, too frozen with fear to move, too shocked to make sense out of the thoughts that flew through her head.

Then something inside her broke loose, and her instincts took over. She turned and ran for Brody's sitting room.

The man lunged at her. He grabbed at her arm and caught a handful of her blouse.

Fabric tore as he jerked her off her feet. She fell back against him, nearly gagging on the hideous smell of his cologne.

"Stop it! Help!" she screamed. "Help! Police!"

A blinding pain slammed into the side of her head.

Her cheek hit the carpet. Dazed, she tried to push herself up and forward, but before she could move, he'd flopped down on top of her and wrapped his big rough hands around her neck.

Déjà vu ripped through her in an adrenaline rush. She bucked and kicked, trying to get him off her, but he was too big, too heavy, too strong.

His fingers squeezed, gagging her. She couldn't breathe.

She scratched at him impotently. Still, she tried.

"Why—?" she rasped.

"*¡Usted es el último, puta!*"

"Last?" she whispered. She was the last what? Victoria had a vague notion that whatever he was saying was important.

As her lungs burned for air and pain blinded her, she threw the last of her strength into pulling herself forward, trying to get away from him.

Something stabbed the underside of her breast.

At first her cloudy brain didn't catch the significance of the stinging pain. His fingers were crushing her throat. No air was getting through. Her lungs were spasming, her heart was racing out of control.

Her breast still stung. With a strangely bright flash of insight she remembered.

The fingernail file! She'd dropped it when she'd fallen. If she could get her hand under her...

Her heart was pounding desperately. Her whole body was screaming for air. Her vision grew black. With what she knew was the last burst of adrenaline in her body, she bowed her back, pushing with more strength than she thought she had against her attacker's bulk.

Her fingers closed around the file.

But her throat hurt, and her head was swimming. She needed to stop, just for a minute, and catch her breath.

Someone was talking but she didn't care.

She couldn't think right now. Her body was collapsing. She'd been without breath for too long. His hands were squeezing too tightly. Any second now her neck was going to snap.

No! She clenched her fists and felt the fingernail file. She was supposed to do something with it.

"Die, *puta!*"

Stars exploded in her eyes, her ears rang. With her last conscious thought, she jabbed the metal file into the hands that were killing her.

Something changed.

He let go, spitting a string of vile curses.

Victoria's chest and throat spasmed, but it was too late. She couldn't get any air. *None.*

She stretched her neck, tried to push herself upright, but she couldn't. She gasped, and felt a tiny whisper of air on the back of her throat, but it wasn't enough.

She collapsed. He'd killed her.

AS SOON AS BRODY rounded the corner of the conference wing of the country club, he saw something wrong. The conference-suite door had a thin stripe of light showing around its edge.

It wasn't locked. He sprinted down the hall and shouldered the door open, drawing his weapon.

The sight in front of him nearly drove him to his knees.

Victoria was crumpled on the floor with Vincent Montoya standing over her, a gun pointed at her head. Montoya's head jerked in Brody's direction, but his gun hand didn't waver.

Every fiber of Brody's being wanted to dive for Vic, to cover her body with his, to protect her from Montoya.

But that would be suicide. And if he died, she surely would, too.

"Montoya! Drop the gun, now!"

Montoya looked up at Brody and shrugged. "It don't matter, Mr. Texas Ranger. She's already dead. I found her like this."

Dead. *No!* "You're a liar," Brody croaked.

"Hey, I'm just trying to help. I think someone choked her. The gun was lying right there."

"Drop it or I'll shoot you right now."

"Now what you want to do that for, Mr. Texas Ranger? I was just trying to help."

"Drop it!"

Montoya's face changed and he swung the gun toward Brody and took a step backward.

In one motion, Brody aimed and shot.

Glass shattered, Montoya screeched and the gun went flying. The chauffeur fell to his knees, clutching his bleeding right hand.

Brody started forward, but Montoya recovered and dove for the gun, which had slid over to the French doors.

In two strides, Brody ground his boot heel into Montoya's wounded hand and put the barrel of his gun against the back of his neck.

"Move and I'll blow your stinking head off," he growled, and racked a bullet into the chamber.

Montoya flattened himself against the floor. "Don't shoot, man. I didn't do nothing!"

Brody's gun barrel shook. His gaze flickered toward Victoria. She still hadn't moved. Dark red streaks stained the side of her neck.

Blood. The sight ratcheted his anger at Montoya up into rage. He put more weight on the man's hand.

Montoya screeched again.

"Move! Make a move!" he growled. "Because I'm dying to watch your brains splatter all over this room."

"Hey, I didn't do nothing—"

"Brody!"

Shock sizzled through him like lightning. His index finger tightened reflexively, and he felt the trigger give.

"Brody, I got him." It was Egan.

Carefully, slowly, Brody relaxed his hand. Egan put a hand on his shoulder for a split second. Then he took Brody's place and wrenched Montoya's hands behind his back, paying no attention to his squeals about brutality.

Egan jerked Montoya to his feet and shoved him toward two uniformed officers. "Get him out of here."

Brody looked down at his gun, ejected the chambered bullet, and then slid it back into its holster.

Victoria! He fell to his knees by her side and gently turned her over. Her eyelids fluttered.

His heart twisted in relief. *She was alive.*

His fingers hovered over her face and neck, where angry red marks were already turning purple.

"Vic, can you hear me? Can you talk?"

She stiffened. Her eyes opened. They were dilated with fear. Then she focused on his face.

"Brody." It was nothing more than a movement of her lips. No sound came out.

"Shh. It's okay. You're going to be okay. Get the paramedics!" he yelled. "Vic, where are you hurt? Just your throat?"

"They're on their way, sir," someone said.

His hand hovered over the streaks of blood on her neck. "Vic, is this your blood?"

She closed her eyes.

"Vic, look at me. Where are you hurt? Can you breathe okay? Vic?"

But she didn't move. He leaned down and listened. Her breaths sounded hoarse, labored, but it sounded like enough air was getting through.

He brushed her hair away from her face and touched the dried blood on her neck. It wasn't hers.

Montoya was still yelling about brutality and assault when the officers hauled him out of the room.

"He'll live to stand trial," Egan said. "Riviera's going to need stitches where Montoya brained him. They're taking both of them to the hospital in the police car. How's Vic?"

Brody let his index finger brush her cheek.

"Brody?" Egan again.

"Where are the damn paramedics?" Just as Brody said it two emergency medical technicians burst in.

"What have we got here?" one of them said as the other brushed Brody aside and knelt beside Victoria.

"She—"

"It's her throat. She was strangled," Egan said.

Brody felt a hand on his arm, pulling him out of the way so the EMTs could examine Victoria.

"She's got blood on her neck," one EMT said to the other. "I don't see a wound."

"Look at her hand," Brody said. "I think she—" He had to stop. His voice wouldn't work anymore. He'd been too late. He'd promised her he'd keep her safe and he'd failed.

"She stabbed him." The EMT pointed. "Look at what she's holding. It's a metal fingernail file with a sharp point."

Dear God, he prayed silently, *thank you for making her so brave.*

If she hadn't managed to stab Montoya with that little fingernail file, the scumbag would have killed her.

The EMTs fixed an oxygen mask over her face and lifted her onto the gurney.

She moaned.

"Be careful, dammit."

The EMTs ignored him. They left, pushing the gurney.

"Brody, go with her." Egan laid his hand on Brody's shoulder.

He shrugged it off. "No. This is my crime scene. I've got to process it."

"Hayes is on his way right now. Believe it or not, we can handle this."

"I said *no.*"

Hayes walked in just in front of the crime-scene investigators. "Everything okay here?"

Brody acknowledged him with a nod. "Start here," he said to the lead CSI. "All the blood should be Montoya's. This is where he strangled Vic—" His throat spasmed.

Dammit, what was the matter with him? Had he lost his nerve?

"Lieutenant McQuade," Egan said, "go to the hospital with Victoria. Sergeant Keller and I can handle it here."

Brody looked at Egan, then at Hayes. He itched to hit something or someone, but they'd taken Montoya away.

"Whoa, Brody," Hayes said, holding up his hands, palms out. "We're the good guys, remember?"

Egan clapped Brody on the shoulder. "They're taking Montoya to the same hospital. You're going to want to escort him to lockup, anyhow."

Yeah. He was. He nodded and headed for the door.

Behind him, he heard Hayes. "Damn. What's the matter with him?"

"I'm afraid Brody McQuade is in love."

Chapter Fourteen

Victoria's throat hurt really badly. She tried to touch her neck, but her hand wouldn't move. She opened her eyes, and gasped.

She was in a hospital room. The realization was instinctive. She'd never been a patient in the hospital before, but the low lights, the nearly silent beeping that reverberated in her head, and the smell of disinfectant and alcohol was unmistakable.

She wasn't dead. The quiet beeping sped up.

The last thing she remembered was stabbing at the man's hand with the fingernail file. She'd stopped him from choking her, but it was too late. Even with his hands gone, she still couldn't breathe.

The last thing she remembered was giving in to death.

No. Her pulse leaped and the beeping surged for an instant. That wasn't the last thing.

The last thing she remembered was Brody's voice.

She took a deep breath and whimpered a little when the harsh air hit her throat. Something tickled her nostrils. It was an oxygen tube. She felt the plastic tube running across her cheeks and the two little nipplelike bits of rubber stuck up her nose. The dry cold air made her want to cough.

She closed her eyes, but just as she did, she heard a quiet rustle of fabric. Someone was in the room. A nurse?

She turned her head slightly, wincing at the pain in her throat.

It was Brody, sitting beside her in a hard-backed chair. His arms were crossed and his head was bowed. He was asleep. His jaw was dark with stubble, and his eyelashes cast fuzzy shadows on his cheeks. He looked haggard and achingly vulnerable.

Victoria's eyes filled with tears.

He'd saved her. He'd gotten there in time. Somehow she'd known he would never totally trust her safety to someone else.

Then the memory hit her.

Dear heavens. It was Montoya. Fear and nausea swept through her. That sickening cologne. Those beefy, punishing hands. She'd been sure he'd killed her. The beeping sped up again.

She tried to move her arm again, to wipe away the tear that rolled down her cheek, but there was tubing and tape attached to it. An IV.

She laid her head back on the pillow and just watched Brody sleep. From the first time she'd seen him, wild with shock and grief over the death of his sister, she'd known she would never forget him. He was honorable, determined, larger than life.

Another tear fell. So what came after never? Because now that she'd had a glimpse into his heart, seen, if only for a moment, his tender side, his fierce passion, his undying love for his sister, forgetting him was going to be even harder.

She knew what came after never—*ever.* She would never forget him—even until forever.

A sob erupted from her chest before she could stop it. She

pressed her lips together and lifted her free hand to cover her mouth. She didn't want to wake him. He looked so tired.

She discovered her heart ached more than her throat did.

Brody stirred. His head shot up and his black eyes zeroed in on her face. "Vic? You okay?"

Stupidly his words brought more tears. She nodded.

He shot up, nearly knocking the chair backward, his face drawn and etched with worry. "I'll get the nurse."

"No," she managed. Her voice was gone. The only sound she could make was a feeble whisper.

"What's the matter? Are you hurting? The nurse is right out there—"

"Brody, stop." She held up her hand and tried to smile.

His gaze roamed over her face and neck.

After a few seconds he relaxed. "You're sure? No, don't talk."

She nodded. "What happened?" she mouthed, her hand touching her bruised throat. "It was Vincent Montoya?" Every word was painful, but she had to know.

"Please, Vic, stop talking. I'll tell you." He grabbed the chair and pulled it closer to the bed. He sat and took her hand in his.

"It *was* Montoya, Kenneth Sutton's driver. We've tracked down the owner of the car that rammed you. The driver of the Ferrari saw part of the license plate. He remembered it because it was 666. It was Montoya's girlfriend's car that killed Kimmie."

Victoria squeezed his hand.

"Best we can figure, he rammed Caroline Stallings's car on purpose. Montoya won't say, Stallings apparently has total amnesia regarding the event, so she can't tell us anything."

Unbearable sadness clouded Brody's face and bowed his

shoulders. Victoria wanted to take him into her arms, but she had to settle for holding on to his hand.

"The break-ins at the condos were a cover-up. He admitted that he went after Zelke and Briggs and you because he thought you'd seen him that night."

Seen him? She hadn't seen anything. She'd been concentrating on her driving. She shook her head.

"I know you didn't. But Montoya couldn't take that chance. The Ranger lab already examined the angle of impact on Caroline Stallings's vehicle and determined that the car came out of a side street. We've got the paint samples. As soon as we turn up the car, we can prove it's the one that killed Kimmie."

"Why?"

"That's what we can't figure out. Everything else is falling into place. My sergeant got a hit on the print they lifted off the humidor. The partial from your neck matched Montoya. But he's decided to lawyer up." Brody shook his head. "I figure someone tipped him off that we were on to him, and that's when he decided he had to get to you. He couldn't take the chance that you'd seen him that night."

Victoria closed her eyes.

"Vic. Get some sleep. You're safe now. We've got him. He's having surgery on his hand this morning, and then he goes straight to lockup. He's got three deaths on his hands, plus an eyewitness—you. He'll never see this side of a cell again."

A quiet knock sounded on the door. Before Brody could slip his hand from Victoria's, Egan stuck his head in.

"Hey, how's she doing?"

Brody had no trouble reading the look in his sergeant's eyes. "She's okay. Any news?"

"Deason's men tracked down the girlfriend, Eleana. She's apparently on a plane to San Diego. Deason called me to let me know she used a credit card at the airport."

"Did they find her car?"

"Yep. We've impounded it, and CSI techs will compare the paint with the samples we've got."

"Get Hayes to work with them."

"He's already there. With the paint samples we got from Montoya's body shop, and the scrapings from Victoria's and Caroline Stallings's cars, I think we can prove it was used in both attacks." Egan stepped into the room and took a look at Victoria. Then he eyed Brody again, a frown on his face.

"Man, you look worse than she does."

"Thanks," Brody said wryly, glancing at her. He couldn't stop a small smile from curving his lips. "Vic's tough. A lot tougher than she looks."

"Right, I see."

He met Egan's gaze and frowned. Why was Egan looking at him like that? "What the hell's wrong with you?" he asked.

"Me? Nothing's wrong with me. We've been wondering what's wrong with *you*. But I think we've figured it out."

Brody remembered what he'd heard as he'd sprinted to catch up with the EMTs. He wasn't going there, not even in his own head, certainly not with Egan.

"Where'd you say Eleana went? San Diego?"

Egan nodded.

"Dammit. We're going to need her to testify that Montoya had access to her car. And that she was the one who gave him access to the condos and the country club."

"We'll get her." Egan ran his hand over his short dark hair. "I think Montoya's going into surgery in about an hour or so."

Brody looked at his watch. "It's almost 6:00 a.m."

"Yep. It's been a long night. I'm headed over to pay a visit to Kenneth Sutton. I'm pulling him in for questioning."

"Good. What about Carlson?"

"That weasel? He's still cooling his heels in an interrogation room." Egan laughed. "He practically peed his pants when we brought him in."

"Has he got an explanation for how his prints got on that humidor? According to Vic, Dalloway polished it every damn day."

"He claims Dalloway wanted to sell it. That's all he'll say."

"Lean on him. He'll crack. He came very close to threatening Vic one night. Besides, he seems to gravitate toward lowlifes. He's driving a fairly new BMW—"

"And Montoya's got that chop shop. I'll make sure to check on his registration and the vehicle ID number."

"Good deal, thanks."

Victoria stirred and Brody stepped over and took her hand.

"Brody…" Egan said.

Brody leveled a glare at the sergeant. "Yeah?"

"She's a prize."

He frowned at his friend, about to throw out a flippant remark. But at that instant Victoria made a small sound, as if she was hurting, and his heart squeezed in his chest, making it impossible to speak.

He swallowed and nodded.

"See you later, Lieutenant."

Brody took a deep breath and sat back down beside Victoria. Her neck was blotchy with dark purple and angry yellow ovals, where Montoya had bruised her with his fingers.

Brody's trigger finger twitched, and he recalled just how close he'd been to pulling that trigger. He'd never consciously thought about killing anyone before, but in that moment, when he'd seen Montoya standing over her with his gun aimed at her head, Brody could have killed him.

BRODY'S CELL PHONE VIBRATED. He realized he'd been watching Victoria sleep. He glanced at the clock opposite her bed. After seven. Then he looked at his phone. It was Deason.

He walked out into the hall before he answered.

"Lieutenant, Montoya's gone."

"What? What the hell?" Brody sprinted toward the elevator, dodging a nurse with a medication cart and a maintenance woman mopping up a spill. "When? Why didn't they call me?"

"The nurse's aid left him on a gurney in the hall, waiting to go into surgery. When he came back to roll him in, Montoya was gone. He was medicated."

"How long's he been gone?"

"At least half an hour. I've got officers rounding up the hospital's security guards. They're watching all the exits and mounting a search."

"It's too late for that."

"I know but—"

"We've got to do it," Brody said. "I'm heading over to his house."

"I've got a plainclothes officer already there. The second Montoya shows up, we'll know it."

TWO HOURS LATER Brody stood in a rented warehouse near downtown San Antonio, staring down at Montoya's body slumped over a scratched wooden desk. A small black hole marred the side of the man's face. His other cheek lay in a pool of blood that dripped off the edge of the desk.

"Get a close-up of that," Brody said, pointing to the entrance wound.

The CSI technician aimed the digital camera and snapped a shot, then a second one. "Powder burns," the tech said.

Brody nodded. "Whoever did this, Montoya knew them, and was comfortable enough to turn his back to them." He looked around for Deason. The Detective Sergeant was talking with an officer over by the side door.

When Brody walked up, Deason was examining the door's lock.

"The door wasn't forced," the officer was saying. "And it appears it wasn't even locked."

"Is someone looking at the tire tracks outside?" Brody asked. "Whoever killed him came here for that purpose. This was an execution. Somebody was afraid Montoya was going to talk."

"Brody! Come take a look at this," Egan called. He was on the far side of the building, standing at a counter that appeared to serve as a snack area.

Brody strode across the width of the building, marveling at how clean it was. There didn't seem to be a speck of dust anywhere, and certainly not on either of the three cars that were lined up in front of the massive rolling door.

"We found two beer bottles in the trash. We're bagging them, but look at this." Egan pointed to the various cups and mugs and glasses lined up beside the sink. "All of them are bone dry, except for this one," he said, indicating a serviceable green ceramic mug. It was sitting facedown, just like the others. But there was a small wet circle on the counter where it sat.

"Is that beer?"

Egan shook his head. "Water."

"Whoever drank that second beer used a glass." Brody commented thoughtfully. "And cleaned up after they shot Montoya. A woman?"

"Well, it's not the girlfriend."

"Nope. We've verified that she's on that plane to San Diego. Besides, I think it's more likely to be a man."

"Yeah." Egan's mouth curled in distaste. "Some rich arrogant prick like Link Hathaway or Kenneth Sutton. I mean, can you see a man who keeps a *chauffeur* drinking beer out of a bottle?"

Brody frowned at him and shook his head. "So we're looking at every person, male or female, Montoya ever came in contact with, especially in Cantara Hills. But considering the circles Sutton and Hathaway ran in, conceivably all over the city."

"At least that narrows it down from everybody in the known universe."

Deason walked up in time to hear Brody's comment. "What about his ties to car theft and chopping?"

"It's possible, but the way this looks, and the fact that it happened right now, makes me think it's got to be connected with his murder spree."

"Somebody was afraid he'd try to cut a deal—that he'd talk." Egan glanced over at the body. "Guess he won't tell us anything now."

"Whoever killed him is going to be worried about the same thing he was—that Vic saw something. She could still be in danger. I need you to take over the case, Egan. I want to get Vic out of here. I'm thinking Eleana knows something about Montoya's contacts. She might even know who killed him. I'm going to find her and question her. And I'm taking Vic with me. Then I'll set her up in protective custody until we solve this thing."

"You're leaving me with a murderer's fresh corpse and a city full of suspects?"

Brody clapped his sergeant on the back. "If there's one thing I'm sure of, Caldwell, it's that you can handle it."

"Right," Egan said wryly. "Thanks for the vote of confidence."

Epilogue

That afternoon Brody was able to take Victoria home. Her voice was still hoarse, and angry fresh bruises stood out against the older ones on her neck, but she was thrilled to be out of the hospital, and Brody was glad to have her out.

He gave her one of the tablets the doctor had prescribed and put her to bed. He sat down beside her. There was no way she'd be out of his sight ever again—not until he could be sure she was safe. He took her hand in his.

If he was right, and he was certain he was, whoever had killed Montoya was connected with his sister's death eight months before. If Montoya had been afraid Vic had seen him, then whoever killed him was probably worried about the same thing. She wouldn't be completely safe until the person who'd murdered Montoya to keep him from talking was caught.

"Mmm." Victoria moaned and opened her eyes.

Damn. He'd squeezed her hand too hard. "Sorry," he whispered. "Go back to sleep."

She looked at him and smiled. It was a tiny little smile, but it sent an arrow of something really painful straight to his heart.

"I'm tired of sleeping," she whispered. Her voice was a little bit stronger. "Besides, people keep waking me up."

"Sorry."

"Stop saying that, Brody." She pushed herself up in the bed. "Can I have some water?"

"Sure." He let go of her hand and reached for a bottle he'd set beside the bed earlier. He tried to hold it for her, but she took it from his fingers.

"Thank you." She closed her eyes. "Brody? Why are you here?"

"I…uh…"

She opened her eyes to narrow slits. "Lieutenant McQuade speechless?"

Brody clenched his jaw. What was he going to say to her? That he couldn't bear to let her out of his sight? That he feared that if he left her side for one second something could happen?

While he was thinking that, her eyes drifted closed again and her breathing evened out. She'd gone to sleep.

He took the bottle of water and set it on the bedside table and took her hand in his again. Something he'd never felt before made him lean over and press his lips to her fingers. Then he pressed her hand to his cheek.

"Brody?"

He jumped and let go of her hand.

"Why didn't you tell me about your inheritance? I assume from your parents."

Her words sliced through him. He swallowed. How did she…? Suddenly he remembered the envelope he'd left sitting on the side table.

"I never wanted that money. It's blood money. Having too much money killed my parents."

She nodded. "I know. It killed my fiancé, too."

Brody stared at her. She *did* know. "Vic, I'm sorry. I should have come clean."

Her hand went to her throat and her green eyes looked at him steadily. "Yes, you should have. You know it's not money that's the root of evil. It's the *love* of money."

"Yeah."

"What are you going to do with it?"

He wiped a hand over his face. "What do you mean?"

"I saw the note. You'd given it all to Kimberly, hadn't you?"

"Put it in trust. She actually was the trust-fund baby." He smiled ruefully. "As to what I'm going to do with it, I'll probably start a scholarship to let people who can't afford it go to law school."

Vic nodded sadly. She rested her hand on his knee and patted it comfortingly.

She was so good, so trusting. *What will I do when you're gone?*

"Good question," she said.

"What?" His head shot up.

She squeezed his knee. "I've been wondering the same thing," she whispered.

"Wondering?"

She raised her brows. "What I'm going to do when you're gone. So I decided that it doesn't bear thinking about. So…"

Brody realized he was holding his breath. And that his heart was pounding like mad. "So…"

"This is really hard for me—not because of my throat." She sent him a tentative grin. "I don't suppose you could help me out here?"

Brody didn't think he could talk, but he knew he had to try. "Vic, do you…would you…"

Her grin grew wider.

"…want to, that is…?"

Her green eyes sparkled.

He took a deep breath. "M-marry me?"

She reached out and touched his cheek. "It would be my great honor and pleasure."

"Vic, I…I'm…really bad at this. I've never done it before." He felt his face heat up. "But…I love you."

"That was very brave of you," she said.

"It was a lot harder than chasing bad guys."

She laughed.

He couldn't help it. Her laughter swirled through him like a summer breeze, lifting his spirits and making him want to laugh, too, for the first time in eight months.

Victoria's eyes lit up and she placed her hand on his chest.

"What now?" he asked, covering her hand with his.

"Feel that rumbling?"

"That's me laughing." He chuckled.

"That's your heart, Brody McQuade."

* * * * *

*The Silver Star of Texas: Cantara Hills Investigation
continues next month!
Don't miss Delores Fossen's
QUESTIONING THE HEIRESS,
only in Harlequin Intrigue.*

The editors at Harlequin Blaze have never been afraid to push the limits   tempting readers with the forbidden, whetting their appetites with a wide variety of story lines. But now we're breaking the final barrier—the time barrier.

In July, watch for BOUND TO PLEASE by fan favorite Hope Tarr, Harlequin Blaze's first ever *historical romance*—a story that's truly Blaze-worthy in every sense.

Here's a sneak peek...

Brianna stretched out beside Ewan, languid as a cat, and promptly fell asleep. Midday sunshine streamed into the chamber, bathing her lovely, long-limbed body in golden light, the sea-scented breeze wafting inside to dry the damp red-gold tendrils curling about her flushed face. Propping himself up on one elbow, Ewan slid his gaze over her. She looked beautiful and whole, satisfied and sated, and altogether happier than he had so far seen her. A slight smile curved her beautiful lips as though she must be in the midst of a lovely dream. She'd molded her lush, lovely body to his and laid her head in the curve of his shoulder and settled in to sleep beside him. For the longest while he lay there turned toward her, content to watch her sleep, at near perfect peace.

Not wholly perfect, for she had yet to answer his marriage proposal. Still, she wanted to make a baby with him, and Ewan no longer viewed her plan as the travesty he once had. He wanted children—sons to carry on after him, though a bonny little daughter with flame-colored hair would be nice, too. But he also wanted more than to simply plant his seed and be on his way. He wanted to lie beside Brianna night upon night as she increased, rub soothing unguents into the swell of her belly, knead the ache from her back and make slow, gentle love to her. He wanted to hold his newly born child in his arms and look down into Brianna's tired but radiant face and blot the perspiration from her brow and be a husband to her in every way.

He gave her a gentle nudge. "Brie?"

"Hmmm?"

She rolled onto her side and he captured her against his chest. One arm wrapped about her waist, he bent to her ear and asked, "Do you think we might have just made a baby?"

Her eyes remained closed, but he felt her tense against him. "I don't know. We'll have to wait and see."

He stroked his hand over the flat plane of her belly. "You're so small and tight it's hard to imagine you increasing."

"All women increase no matter how large or small they start out. I may not grow big as a croft, but I'll be big enough, though I have hopes I may not waddle like a duck, at least not too badly."

The reference to his fair-day teasing was not lost on him. He grinned. "Brianna MacLeod grown so large she must sit still for once in her life. I'll need the proof of my own eyes to believe it."

Despite their banter, he felt his spirits dip. Assuming they were so blessed, he wouldn't have the chance to see her thus. By then he would be long gone, restored to his clan according to the sad bargain they'd struck. He opened his mouth to ask her to marry him again and then clamped it closed, not wanting to spoil the moment, but the unspoken words weighed like a millstone on his heart.

The damnable bargain they'd struck was proving to be a devil's pact indeed.

* * * * *

Will these two star-crossed lovers find their sexily-ever-after?
Find out in BOUND TO PLEASE by Hope Tarr,
available in July wherever Harlequin® Blaze™
books are sold.

Harlequin Blaze marks new territory with its first historical novel!

For years readers have trusted the Harlequin Blaze series to entertain them with a variety of stories—Now Blaze is breaking down the final barrier—the time barrier!

Welcome to Blaze Historicals—all the sexiness you love in a Blaze novel, all the adventure of a historical romance. It's the best of both worlds!

Don't miss the first book in this exciting new miniseries:

BOUND TO PLEASE
by Hope Tarr

New laird Brianna MacLeod knows she can't protect her land or her people without a man by her side. So what else can she do—she kidnaps one! Only, she doesn't expect to find herself the one enslaved....

Available in July wherever Harlequin books are sold.

HB79411

HARLEQUIN®
Super Romance®

Lawyer Audrey Lincoln has sworn off
love, throwing herself into her work
instead. When she meets a much younger
cop named Ryan Mercedes, all her logic
is tossed out the window, and Ryan is
determined that he will not let the issue
of age come between them. It is not until
a tragic case involving an innocent child
threatens to tear them apart that Ryan
and Audrey must fight for a way to
finally be together....

Look for

TRUSTING RYAN
by Tara Taylor Quinn

*Available July
wherever you buy books.*

REQUEST YOUR FREE BOOKS!

2 FREE NOVELS PLUS 2 FREE GIFTS!

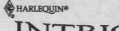

HARLEQUIN®
INTRIGUE®

Breathtaking Romantic Suspense

YES! Please send me 2 FREE Harlequin Intrigue® novels and my 2 FREE gifts (gifts are worth about $10). After receiving them, if I don't wish to receive any more books, I can return the shipping statement marked "cancel." If I don't cancel, I will receive 6 brand-new novels every month and be billed just $4.24 per book in the U.S. or $4.99 per book in Canada, plus 25¢ shipping and handling per book and applicable taxes, if any*. That's a savings of close to 15% off the cover price! I understand that accepting the 2 free books and gifts places me under no obligation to buy anything. I can always return a shipment and cancel at any time. Even if I never buy another book from Harlequin, the two free books and gifts are mine to keep forever.

182 HDN EEZ7 382 HDN EEZK

Name	(PLEASE PRINT)	
Address		Apt. #
City	State/Prov.	Zip/Postal Code

Signature (if under 18, a parent or guardian must sign)

Mail to the **Harlequin Reader Service:**
IN U.S.A.: P.O. Box 1867, Buffalo, NY 14240-1867
IN CANADA: P.O. Box 609, Fort Erie, Ontario L2A 5X3

Not valid to current subscribers of Harlequin Intrigue books.

Want to try two free books from another line?
Call 1-800-873-8635 or visit www.morefreebooks.com.

* Terms and prices subject to change without notice. N.Y. residents add applicable sales tax. Canadian residents will be charged applicable provincial taxes and GST. Offer not valid in Quebec. This offer is limited to one order per household. All orders subject to approval. Credit or debit balances in a customer's account(s) may be offset by any other outstanding balance owed by or to the customer. Please allow 4 to 6 weeks for delivery. Offer available while quantities last.

Your Privacy: Harlequin is committed to protecting your privacy. Our Privacy Policy is available online at www.eHarlequin.com or upon request from the Reader Service. From time to time we make our lists of customers available to reputable third parties who may have a product or service of interest to you. If you would prefer we not share your name and address, please check here. ☐

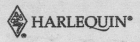

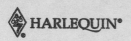 **HARLEQUIN®**

INTRIGUE®
COMING NEXT MONTH

#1071 IDENTITY UNKNOWN by Debra Webb
Colby Agency
Sande Williams woke up in the morgue—left for dead, her identity stolen. Only Colby agent Patrick O'Brien can set Sande's life straight, but at what cost does their partnership come?

#1072 SOLDIER CAGED by Rebecca York
43 Light Street
Kept under surveillence in a secret, military bunker, Jonah Baker is a damaged war hero looking for a way out. Sophia Rhodes may be the one doctor he can bend to his will, but their escape is only the first step in stopping this dangerous charade.

#1073 ARMED AND DEVASTATING by Julie Miller
The Precinct: Brotherhood of the Badge
Det. Atticus Kincaid knows more about solving crimes than charming ladies. But he'll do whatever it takes—even turn quiet Brooke Hansford into an irresistible investigator—to solve a very personal murder case, no matter the family secrets it unearths.

#1074 IN THE MANOR WITH THE MILLIONAIRE
by Cassie Miles
The Curse of Raven's Cliff
Madeline Douglas always had dreams of living in the big house. But taking up residence in historic Beacon Manor is the stuff of nightmares, which only the powerful and handsome Blake Monroe can help to overcome.

#1075 QUESTIONING THE HEIRESS by Delores Fossen
The Silver Star of Texas: Cantara Hills Investigation
With three murder victims among her social circle, Caroline Stallings isn't getting invited to many San Antonio events. Texas Ranger Egan Caldwell is the one man returning her calls, only he's spearheading an investigation that may uncover a shared dark past.

#1076 THE LAWMAN'S SECRET SON by Alice Sharpe
Skye Brother Babies
Brady Skye was a disgraced cop working tirelessly to win back his reputation. But only the son he never knew he had can help him piece together his life—and reunite him with his first love, Lara Kirk—before someone takes an eye for an eye.

www.eHarlequin.com

HICNM0608